ESCAPE
to Shadow Creek Ranch

ESCAPE
to Shadow Creek Ranch

Charles Mills

HOUSE

AUTUMN HOUSE® PUBLISHING COMPANY

P.O. Box 1139, Hagerstown, Maryland 21741-1139

This book was
Edited by Raymond H. Woolsey
Designed by Bill Kirstein
Cover illustration: Joe VanSeveren
Cover design by Byron Steele
Type set: 11/12 Century Schoolbook

PRINTED IN U.S.A.

96 95 94 93 92 91   10 9 8 7 6 5 4 3 2 1

AH Cataloging Service
Mills, Charles.
  Escape to Shadow Creek Ranch.

  I. Title.
     813

ISBN 1-878951-13-0

To my wife
DORINDA

Thank you for making
my words and my life better

Contents

CHAPTER ONE

STEEL CANYONS

★ ★ ★

Joey felt his chest tighten as short, painful bursts of air escaped his aching lungs and whistled along his throat. His feet pounded the sidewalk in quick, percussive beats.

Occasionally a dog's bark spilled from a dark alley and chased his speeding form as it moved, phantom-like, through the midnight shadows.

He ran faster and faster until he knew his arms, legs, and chest were working at total capacity, total effort. If those men wanted him they'd have to catch him. It was as simple as that.

A police car skidded around the corner, its flashing lights revealing in blue and red blinks the dark, brooding buildings and the trash cans that littered the street. Determined eyes peered from behind the steering wheel as tires screamed their protest and a siren wailed in the crisp night air.

As he ran, Joey was aware of the hard, metal object

pressing against his stomach. They'd be sure to find it. He'd be in more trouble than ever before. He must not let the men catch him. Not tonight, not ever.

Sergeant Ryan Miller strained against his shoulder harness as the squad car careened around another corner and continued toward the running figure. His partner, Nathan Gabriel, a rookie on the force, nervously glanced down at the speedometer then back out the window.

"Hang on, Nat," Sergeant Miller called above the siren's scream. "We're gaining on him."

"No problem," the young man shouted back as he grabbed his armrest, trying to steady his lurching body. "I've heard you're a good driver. Besides, there's not much traffic around here this time of night."

At that moment a taxicab pulled out from the shadows in front of the police car. Sergeant Miller spun the wheel; his vehicle raced over the curb and onto the sidewalk. Trash cans, cardboard boxes, and awning poles flew high into the air as he rammed them. Miller caught a glimpse of the fire hydrant on the corner just a second before his out-of-control cruiser spun over it.

"Brace yourself!" he shouted.

The car struck the hydrant with enough force to neatly shear it off at sidewalk level. The impact flipped the vehicle over several times; it skidded on its roof and came to rest in the middle of the intersection amid broken glass, bent strips of metal, and leaking gasoline.

Joey heard the sounds of the car's last moments and stopped running. Spinning around he saw a geyser of water erupt from the broken fire hydrant and watched as the cruiser ground to a halt upside-down in the middle of the street.

The boy hesitated. Now was his chance. Now he

could get away before anyone else came.

Suddenly he saw a tiny flicker of light playing near the front of the car. A yellow flame flared somewhere deep inside the engine compartment, its glow reflected in the creeping rivers of gasoline that snaked away from the vehicle and toward the gutter.

Joey's eyes opened wide in horror. Fire. The smashed car was catching on fire! What should he do?

He moved toward the car, his mind agonizing over the decision he must make. Should he run? Should he escape? Or should he try to save the two men trapped inside the car? He could see them now. One was older than the other. They were moving about slowly. The younger man had blood on his face.

The glow from the flames made them look pale, unnatural, almost like they weren't human. Joey's hands began to shake. What should he do?

The older officer caught sight of Joey. He stopped struggling and reached out a hand in his direction. Joey saw the man's lips moving, repeating something over and over. Then he understood. He was saying, "Please, please!" This hunter, this cop, this force who had been chasing him was now asking for mercy.

Joey's fists clenched at his side. Why should he help? No one had ever helped him when he was in trouble. No one ever ran to his rescue. The people who moved in and out of his world looked at him only with scorn, ridicule, or indifference. He hated them. He hated them all. Why should he help someone who would only turn around and hurt him?

A spurt of fuel sent flames boiling into the night air. The car seemed to settle a bit, pressing its occupants closer to the hard, gas-soaked blacktop.

Again the older man looked toward the boy. This time Joey noticed the pleading was gone from the eyes.

It had been replaced with a look of understanding, of acceptance, of resolve.

The boy edged closer to the burning car. Something deep inside himself was driving him toward the two men pinned under the twisted, broken cruiser. His anger was being replaced with a confusing flood of thoughts. If he left the two men to die, he would be acting the same way everyone else acted in his world. He'd be no better than the very people he hated. A sudden chill ran down his spine as he realized that if he ran he'd have to start hating himself too.

"No!" the boy screamed up at the darkened buildings, their occupants entombed behind tightly shut windows and tightly locked doors. No one had ventured out to help the men. No one wanted to get involved with life outside their tiny world. "I will not be like you! I just won't!"

Resolve turned quickly into action. Joey raced to the crumpled squad car and then slithered along the oily road on his stomach.

Reaching the driver's door, he pressed through the shattered window. In moments he'd unlatched the seatbelts that bound the occupants to their seats and slowly, carefully, dragged them one at a time away from the flames.

The fire scorched his hair and jacket but he ignored it. Broken glass and razor-sharp pieces of metal cut deep into his elbows and knees as he worked.

The flames grew larger. Tongues of fire rolled away from the wreck, following the twisting rivers of gas and oil spreading across the intersection.

With a final, straining effort, Joey managed to pull the second man to the curb. As he stood to catch his breath the car's fuel tank exploded in a blinding flash. A searing rush of air picked Joey up off the ground and slammed him through a storefront window. He landed hard against the counter and sprawled over the tiled floor. He felt himself sinking, falling, spinning into darkness. Then, everything was still.

* * * * *

Afternoon traffic ground to a halt as gridlock seized Manhattan for the second time in three days. Horns blared driver frustrations; hot, polluted air rose from the steaming streets and enveloped the tall steel-and-glass fingers that form the famous skyline of New York City's financial district.

High inside one of those structures, a door bearing a hand-lettered sign that read "Hanson & Hanson—Attorneys at Law" swung open.

A tall, dark-haired man wearing a three-piece suit hurriedly entered a plush, richly appointed office suite. He glanced over at a woman who sat behind a reception desk by the window.

"They here?" he asked, throwing his briefcase on a table and flipping it open.

"They were," came the answer. "You just missed them."

The man closed his eyes and let out a long sigh.

"They waited for over an hour," the woman continued. "I told them you'd probably be late, traffic and all, but . . ."

"Thanks, Martha," the man said. "I'm sure you did what you could. I just spent 45 minutes under the Hudson River choking on bus fumes. The Holland Tunnel is getting more and more like a giant tail pipe every day. Oh, well, call their secretaries and set up another meeting. I'll be in my office."

The woman smiled and reached for the phone. Hesitating, she called out, "Oh, Mr. Hanson, your daughter called."

"Which one?"

"Debbie."

The man slipped out of his coat and tossed it over the back of a large leather chair behind his highly polished desk. "What'd she want?"

"I don't know. Something about how the world as we know it will end if you don't call her back right away."

Mr. Hanson smiled. "Sounds serious."

The woman walked to the entrance of the man's office and leaned up against the door frame. "When you're 16, everything's serious."

"Oh, yeah, I forgot," Mr. Hanson laughed quietly to himself. "Life is just one big crisis after another. They think adults couldn't possibly have so many problems." His face saddened just a little. "We have our own endless supply. They'll find out soon enough."

The woman nodded. "Just give her a call. She sounded desperate."

Mr. Hanson waved as he picked up the phone and began dialing. Leaning back in his chair, he waited for his call to go through.

In another part of the city, a phone rang in the living room of an apartment perched high above the crowded streets. A pretty dark-haired teenager jumped up from her homework and raced across the room.

Her sister, 9-year-old Wendy, dropped what she was doing and jumped for the phone too. They collided and toppled over each other, knocking the telephone, the lamp, and a picture of a flower off the end table.

From the tangle of arms and legs, a hand grasped the receiver and a duet of voices called out, "Hello?"

Mr. Hanson heard the ruckus on the other end of the line and rolled his eyes toward the ceiling.

"Will it ever be possible for just one of you to

14

answer the phone when I call?" he pleaded. "Is that too much to ask?"

"Oh, hello, Daddy," a young voice shouted. "Did you want to talk to me?"

"Are you Debbie?"

"Me, Debbie? Yuk! I'm Wendy. Wouldn't you rather talk to me? I'm smarter, you know."

"You are not," another voice countered. "He called for me. I asked him to. Now go away."

"Daddy?" The first voice spoke into the phone. "Is that true? Did she ask you to call her? 'Cause if it's not true I'll talk to you. I got lots of stuff to say."

The man leaned forward in his chair, "Deb . . . , I mean Wendy, Debbie did ask me to call her, so would you please give her the phone."

"Well, OK," came the disappointed reply, "but, come home soon, we're going to have pizza for—"

"Give me that," the other child demanded. After another short tussle, Debbie's clear, sweet voice sounded in the receiver pressed against Mr. Hanson's ear.

"Daddy? I'm so glad you called. I have a problem. No, not just a problem; a great, big, gigantic problem that needs immediate attention."

"OK," the man answered. "Let me have it."

"Well, you know Macy's Department Store?"

"I think I've heard of it. They have a parade each year, don't they?"

"Yeah . . . well . . . they're having a once-in-a-lifetime, get-it-now-before-they're-gone, he-who-hesitates-is-lost, prices-to-die-for sale in their junior department and you know that red coat I showed you a picture of in the catalog, you know, the one that has that furry hat that comes with it and those gloves you can get for half price if you buy the coat? Do you remember?"

Mr. Hanson blinked twice. "Uh, I think so."

"Well, it's on sale! Can you believe it? Thirty-five percent off! I mean, this is such a deal. Like, if we don't go buy this coat, we'll be sorry forever."

"We will?"

"Absolutely. So is it all right?"

The man cleared his throat. "What about your other coat—the one I bought you last year? It looks great on you."

"Dad!" Mr. Hanson knew that what was to follow would be of utmost importance. Debbie only called him "Dad" if the end of the world was at stake.

"Dad," the voice on the line repeated, "that's a lovely coat and I really, really appreciate you getting it for me, but—"

The man waited.

"But, it's old."

"What do you mean it's old?" Mr. Hanson queried. "I just bought it last year!"

Debbie sighed. "I don't mean *old* old, I mean . . . *looks* old. It looks like . . . last year. You know what I mean?"

"No."

"That coat was fine for last year, but, this year . . . well . . . the sleeves are all wrong."

Mr. Hanson closed his eyes and ran a hand through his thick, dark hair. "The sleeves are all wrong? What are they, backwards?"

Debbie giggled, her soft brown eyes sparkling. "No, they're not backwards. Oh, you don't understand fashion. Can I go get the coat? You'll think I'm so beautiful in it."

The man smiled. "I think you're so beautiful in last

16

year's coat. But, if it means that much to you, tell Mr. Simmons to charge it to our account."

"Oh, Daddy," the voice on the line squealed, "you're the most wonderful, most generous, most handsomest, kindest, greatest . . ."

"Yeah, yeah, yeah," the man interrupted. "Just be back by 6:00. Take your sister with you. Goodbye."

"I love you, Daddy," the girl said softly. "I love you."

The man heard the phone click onto its cradle and a low hum return to the line. He gently placed his receiver on its hook and glanced up toward the door. Martha was standing there, a smile spreading across her face.

"You're a weak man, Tyler Hanson," she spoke quietly. "But, I'll give you one thing. You do love those two young ladies waiting for you at home. They can wrap you around their little fingers faster than a gunslinger can twirl his six-shooter."

"Guilty," the man admitted, lifting his hands above his head. "Guilty as charged."

The woman nodded, then placed a file folder on the desk. "This should make your day. It's from Captain Abernathy on the Lower East Side. They had a little action last night on First Avenue. Made quite a mess, I hear. Some juvenile involved. He said that you may have the privilege of representing the kid."

"Sometimes I think Abernathy is a mindreader," Mr. Hanson groaned, shaking his head in disbelief while studying the contents of the folder. "How'd he know it was time for us to take on another charity case? My dad always said the man was psychic."

Martha laughed. "Well, I think it's very nice that a firm like Hanson & Hanson doesn't forget the fact that poor people need legal assistance, too. You and your dad have helped a lot of folk through the years. You're a rare breed of lawyer."

Mr. Hanson sighed. "Getting someone out of trouble is one thing. Keeping them out is another matter all together. Putting innocent people back out on these streets can be as much a punishment as throwing them behind bars. I don't know. We do what we can."

Mr. Hanson stood, flipped the folder shut, and began tossing papers into his briefcase. "I'll spend the rest of the afternoon on this case. If you need me, call my beeper."

At the door he paused. "Oh, and if Wendy phones, tell her just because her sister is getting a new coat doesn't mean she suddenly needs one too."

With a wave he was gone. Martha chuckled, then turned and walked back to her desk by the window.

The traffic situation hadn't improved any as Mr. Hanson exited the building, so he made his way to a nearby subway station and pressed in among the crowds headed for wherever New Yorkers go on hot summer afternoons.

Thirty-five minutes later, Tyler Hanson stood facing a tall, white-dressed nurse in a busy East Side hospital. He had to almost shout to be heard over the commotion that swirled in and around the nurses' station.

"I'm here to see a—" he flipped open his folder and read the name printed on the police report, "a Joey Dugan. He was brought in last night."

"Who?" the nurse asked without looking up. She continued typing on an old manual typewriter balanced on a stack of papers.

"Dugan, Joey Dugan," Mr. Hanson repeated, "15 years old—uh—police file number 13472 dash A, Third Precinct, Captain Abernathy. Admitted around 1:00

18

a.m. Car accident. Banged up pretty bad. Is he here?"

The nurse was too busy to help much. "Look around," she said. "See for yourself. He'd probably still be up in recovery. Third floor. Take the stairs. Elevator's busted."

"Thanks," Mr. Hanson called out, absorbed by the flow of activity spilling down the hallway that led in the direction the nurse had pointed. The woman returned to her typing.

The third floor was considerably quieter than the first and the charge nurse said she knew where the Dugan boy was. She led the visitor to a small room near the fire exit.

"He's a mess," the nurse said. "Nothing broken though. The doctor says he must be one tough kid. Try not to excite him." The woman turned to continue her rounds.

Mr. Hanson stood in the doorway, looking at the still form on the bed. Hanging from a tall, stainless steel pipe, an IV bag dripped silently, sending its life-sustaining fluid down a clear plastic tube to the boy's arm. White bandages surrounded the young face and wrapped themselves around sections of the lad's arms and legs. His knees and elbows had received extra portions of the soft, protective covering.

Another tube ran from the boy's nose to a machine that rested against the wall.

Red and blue wires connected the lad's chest with a heart monitor placed beside the bed. Across the machine's tiny screen the man saw an electrically created line jump rhythmically; a soft beeping sound informed whoever was interested that the boy's heart was still beating. Otherwise the small room was empty and completely silent.

"Joey?" Mr. Hanson called softly. "Joey Dugan?"

The boy opened his eyes and stared at the stranger standing in the doorway. He blinked several times, then closed his eyes again.

"Who are you?" he said.

"I'm Mr. Hanson. Captain Abernathy asked me to serve as council on your behalf."

"He asked you to what?"

"He asked me to be your lawyer."

"Hey man, do I look like someone who could afford a hotshot lawyer like you? Get real."

Mr. Hanson edged into the room. "No, there'll be no charge. It won't cost you anything."

Joey looked at the man coldly. "How generous of you."

Mr. Hanson cleared his throat. "Yes, well, I need some information. Are you up to talking about last night?"

"Well, I'll have to check my calendar, but I think I can squeeze you in."

The man looked down at the floor then back at the boy. "You're not going to make this easy, are you? All I want to do is help."

There was an honesty in the stranger's voice that made Joey feel a little uncomfortable. Trusting people was something you learned not to do on the streets of the Lower East Side. Those you trusted had a nasty habit of turning around and stabbing you in the back.

But here was a man who looked and acted like a nice guy. His eyes were kind. His manner gentle. Kindness and gentleness seemed out of place in the boy's world.

"So, uh—" Joey studied the man's face, "what'd ya want to know?"

Mr. Hanson reached into his briefcase and pulled out a pad and paper. "The police report said a couple of officers were transporting you along . . . let's see . . . East 12th Street. It says . . ." Hanson picked up the report and read out loud: "The police vehicle suddenly ran up onto the sidewalk, hit a fire hydrant, and then flipped over in the middle of the intersection of East 12th and First Avenue. In the ensuing explosion and fire, the boy was injured along with the two occupants of the car, Sergeant Ryan Miller and Nat Gabriel. The department suggests that the boy, Joey Dugan, may have been the cause of the accident."

Joey let out a long sigh. "That what it says?"

"Yes."

"Then that's what happened."

"But I don't understand something." Mr. Hanson studied the report carefully. "It says here you were found inside a store, and the two officers were lying by the curb. A crashing, burning car doesn't neatly deposit its occupants side by side on the street. Besides, the direction the car was traveling and the position of the wreck indicates that the occupants would be thrown in the opposite direction. It just doesn't make sense."

Joey turned his face to the wall. "Hey, man, if that report says one thing and I say another, who they gonna believe, huh? Me? Sure."

"So this isn't the way it happened?" Mr. Hanson pressed closer to the boy lying on the bed. "Joey, you can't expect the legal system to work for you until the truth is known."

The boy closed his eyes. "Look. I appreciate what you're trying to do. But, like I said, I'm just Joey Dugan, a bad kid from East Village. I learned a long time ago not to make waves. So I'll take my punishment like a man and go on. I ain't got no system working for me. I'm a survivor, and sometimes that means surviving other people's systems."

"Joey," the man countered, "truth is the only defense we have. I need to know—did you or did you not cause the accident?"

The room was silent for a long moment. Footsteps sounded out in the hall then faded away. Mr. Hanson noticed a tear slide silently down the teenager's face. His eyes remained closed. The boy's hands grew limp as he let out a deep sigh.

"For what it's worth," he said softly, "I didn't make the accident happen. I wasn't even in the car. But no one will believe me. I can't prove it."

"You won't have to," a voice called out from the doorway. Joey and Mr. Hanson looked up in surprise. They saw a tall, grey-haired man standing there, his muscular frame supported by a pair of crutches. He wore a bandage wrapped tightly around his forehead. Painfully he hobbled into the room and stood at the foot of Joey's bed.

"I just read the report myself. That's not how it happened. The officer who wrote it was only guessing." The stranger looked down at the boy. "But we know what really happened, don't we?"

"Do I know you?" Joey asked, his voice almost a whisper.

"The name's Miller. Sergeant Ryan Miller. I was the driver of the car that crashed." Turning to Mr. Hanson, he continued. "The boy saved my life and the life of my partner. That's the truth, and I'm willing to tell my story in court."

Mr. Hanson smiled broadly. "Yes. That would be very helpful indeed. Thank you."

"Sergeant Miller?" Joey looked up at the man standing at the foot of his bed.

"Yes?"

"You thought I was gonna leave you there, didn't you?"

The older man nodded slowly. "Yes, I did."

"You weren't mad?"

The sergeant turned and sat down carefully on the bed. "There was a time when I would have been, when I would think how terrible it is for a young man like yourself to turn his back on a fellow human being in distress. But, that was before five years ago."

"What happened?" Joey asked.

"My son Jake stopped to help a stranded motorist out on the Williamsburg Bridge. He was coming home from work, and this man and woman flagged him down and said their car wouldn't start. He gave them a lift into Brooklyn. For his trouble, they stole his wallet, hit him over the head, and threw him into a dumpster. He almost died.

"A few days later, his car was spotted abandoned on the Pennsylvania Turnpike near Pittsburgh. So I really can't blame a guy for not sticking out his neck for someone else."

The big policeman glanced over at Mr. Hanson. "I know it's a rotten way to live your life, but it's safe. A few bad apples are making it hard on the rest of us. That's reality."

Mr. Hanson studied the older man's face for a long moment, then spoke slowly, deliberately. "I'm sorry about your son, Sergeant Miller, but, I don't believe you mean what you just said. You can't think that way and be in the type of work you're in. You put yourself on the line for others every single day. I believe you do it because you don't want people to think that helping isn't worth the risk."

The lawyer paused and motioned toward Joey. "Both you and this young man are living proof that the result is worth the risk in a vast majority of cases."

The policeman sighed. "Tell me something. Why should it be so hard to love other people?"

Mr. Hanson shook his head. "I don't know. Maybe in these steel canyons where we all live, love has been buried under years of fear, misunderstanding, uncertainty. But last night, Joey showed you not everyone believes the lie. Maybe, in your eyes, he saw that you didn't either."

The older man rose slowly, working to balance himself between his crutches. "Get well, son," he said. "And listen to this man. He may be right, even though he looks like he just stepped out of one of Saks Fifth Avenue's fashion windows."

The boy snickered. "Yeah, I'll listen."

Another police officer appeared at the door. Mr. Hanson recognized his friend Captain Abernathy.

"Well, Ted," he said good naturedly, "you come to join the party?"

The captain didn't respond. He walked directly to the bedside and spoke to the patient. "Joey Dugan, you're under arrest for the murder of Li Fong, owner of Fong's Chinese Foods."

"What?" Joey said, trying to sit up in bed, only to be yanked back by the tubes and wires attached to his body.

"What are you saying?" Mr. Hanson pleaded. "What makes you think he killed anyone?"

"This." The captain held up a plastic bag. "We found this gun in Dugan's jacket last night. Ballistics have proved it was the weapon used to kill Li Fong." Turning to the boy he spoke firmly. "You have the right to remain silent. Anything you say can and will be used against you in a court of law. You have the right—"

Mr. Hanson stood in stunned silence. Was this young boy who had risked his life to save Sergeant Miller a murderer? Had the mean streets and steel canyons of New York City claimed yet another victim?

CHAPTER TWO

"JUST BEYOND MY REACH"

★ ★ ★

Debbie and Wendy sat watching buses, cars, bicycles, and pedestrians flow past their taxicab window. The driver swerved just in time to miss a woman pushing a baby carriage.

"Hey, you want that kid of yours to grow up?" the man yelled at the frightened mother. "Watch where you're going!"

Turning to the girls seated in the back of his cab, he laughed out loud. "Sorry for the rough ride little ladies. Horn's broke."

The two smiled weakly and tried to ignore their driver's constant battle of words with the world outside the vehicle.

"I see you've been shopping," the man said, glancing in his rearview mirror and eyeing the packages neatly stacked in one corner of the backseat. "I take my wife shopping once a month. Can't afford to go more often. She buys stuff she don't need just because it's on sale. What a woman! Like I told her a million times, 'What? You think I'm made of money?' She just tells me to mind my own business. She never listens to me. Does your mother ever listen to your dad?"

The girls looked at each other then back out the window. "Our mother is gone," Debbie said flatly.

"Gone? Gone where?"

No answer.

"My mother went to Jersey once," he persisted. "She hates Jersey. Everybody hates Jersey. The only people who don't hate Jersey are the people who live in Jersey. They hate New York. Sort of balances everything out, you know what I mean?"

Debbie stared at the traffic. "She's gone to Connecticut."

"Hey," the driver said enthusiastically, "Connecticut's good. My brother lives there. He says it's like a garden. Not like Jersey. He hates Jersey too."

Wendy moved forward and crouched just behind the driver's seat, her short, blonde hair brushing against her forehead. "Our mother's not coming back," she said.

"Wendy!" Debbie snapped. "Sit down."

"Oh," the driver sympathized, "I'm sorry. Run away, did she? I have a cousin whose wife ran away. He came home one night and said, 'What's for supper?' and no one answered. That was . . . let's see . . . about four years ago. He says if he ever runs into her again, he's going to tell her to leave town."

"Our mother lives with a bank president," Wendy reported.

Debbie looked sternly at her sister. "Be quiet, Wendy."

27

"A bank president?" The taxi driver rubbed his stubble-studded chin. "We ain't got no bank presidents in our family. It's a shame anyway, your mother running off and all. Maybe she'll come back. You never know."

"She's not coming back," Debbie said coldly. "She's not welcome at our house."

"Yes, she is," Wendy insisted. "She can come back anytime she wants. It's OK with me."

"It's not your decision to make," the older girl announced. Then she sighed. "Oh, you don't know anything. You're too little."

"I am not!" the younger argued, her eyes flashing. "I'm 9 years old. That's old enough to know lots of things."

The taxi lurched to a halt at the base of a towering apartment building. "Here you are," the driver said, "back safe and sound. I'm really sorry about your mom."

"Don't be," Debbie said, handing the man a small pile of dollar bills and stepping out onto the sidewalk. "Everything's just fine the way it is."

The driver shrugged and counted the money. "Whatever you say, little lady." Then he eased his cab into the rush of traffic and disappeared around the corner.

The sisters entered the building through tall glass doors and moved across the high-ceilinged lobby. "I don't know why you think Mom will ever come crawling back to Daddy," Debbie said as they headed for the elevators. "She doesn't care about anyone but herself."

"Well, I still miss her," the younger sighed, "even if you don't."

Debbie didn't answer. She pressed number 21 on the silver panel and leaned back against the mirrored surface of the elevator cab. The doors slid shut and with a whoosh the girls felt themselves being carried up, up, up to their home high above the streets of Manhattan.

That night when Mr. Hanson arrived at the apartment he was greeted by two smiling faces and a generous donation of hugs. Debbie treated him to a fashion show, starring a new red coat with "correct" sleeves, a smart, neatly cut fur hat, and matching pair of gloves.

Not to be outdone, Wendy paraded by, her short, stocky frame wrapped in her favorite winter coat but with something added. On the sleeve was a hand-drawn price tag, neatly lettered to show a dollar amount twice as much as Debbie's coat had cost.

"It was on sale too," she reported. "Thousand percent off. And it came with this wonderful matching baseball glove."

Dad was impressed and praised her for her smart "shopping."

How lovely Debbie looked in her new coat. Mr. Hanson admired her fluid movements and the almost professional way she modeled her latest purchase. The young girl's shining hair swung across her shoulders as she danced around the room, turning and twisting her slender body so as to show off each detail of her attire. "You were right," he admitted, taking his daughter in his arms and planting a big kiss on her forehead. "You are beautiful in your new coat. And the sleeves . . . they're so . . . so . . . unwrong!"

Debbie giggled. "See, I told you."

"And Wendy," Mr. Hanson continued, "you look just stunning in your high-priced coat and baseball glove. It's like they were made for each other."

The younger girl beamed.

After the supper dishes had been cleared, the little family settled down for an evening of relaxation. Wendy positioned herself before the television to watch her favorite program while Debbie began calling all of her friends to explain in minute detail the beauty and fashion statement offered by her new red coat.

Father spread his tired body over a well-worn recliner by the wide bay window in the den. The lights from the city filtered through the double-paned glass and cast an eerie, faded glow around the room.

He looked about, letting his mind drift without direction. But, as always, certain memories surfaced at just such moments to echo sights and sounds from the past.

It was here in this very room he had learned the painful truth about his wife, about her secret trips to Connecticut, her lies, her unfaithfulness. Funny, it seemed so long ago, but it hadn't been. Just 14 months, give or take a few days. She had stood right over there by the bookcase and said she was leaving; to "find her inner self," was the way she'd put it.

Mr. Hanson took in a deep breath and let it out slowly. "Her inner self," he repeated quietly. "How does one lose one's inner self?"

"Daddy?" A gentle voice broke through his reverie and carried him abruptly to the present.

"Debbie," he said smiling. "I didn't see you come in. Have you been here long?"

"No. I just wanted to ask you something."

"Now you need new shoes, right?"

"Oh, Daddy," the girl snickered. "No, I don't need any new shoes. I just wanted to ask you a question."

"OK. Shoot."

The girl seated herself among the shadows at the

30

far end of the room. "Daddy? What would you do if Mother came back?"

The man thought for a long moment. "I don't know. What should I do?"

Debbie stared into the darkness. "I can't forgive her. I just can't."

"I know."

The girl continued. "But maybe I should. Maybe I should want to. I mean, you forgive me when I do stupid things. You don't hate me like I . . ."

Mr. Hanson rose and walked across the room. Kneeling beside his daughter's chair he reached up and brushed strands of hair from her brow. "Sometimes we have to separate our feelings about what happened from our feelings about who was involved. It's all right to hate what your mother did to you, to us, but still love her at the same time. I believe that's what we should do."

"You sound like Grandpa," the girl chuckled. "That's like something he'd say."

"It probably was," the man admitted. "He's a wise man."

The girl was silent for a long moment. "I need her. I need to talk to her about stuff."

"I know you do, sweetheart. I know you do."

"But if she came back, I'd keep remembering what she did and I just couldn't pretend nothing had ever happened."

The man nodded. "This type of hurt runs very deep in a person. Very deep. I don't know what to do about it, either. Believe me, I've tried to figure something out but the answer seems to hide just beyond my reach. It's like, I wake up in the morning and I say to myself, 'I'm not going to think about Ellen today. I'm just not going to.' Then a couple hours later, something reminds me of her and . . . well . . . I hurt all over again."

The girl gazed into her father's eyes. "Do you love me, Daddy?"

"You know I do," the man answered, his voice choked.

Debbie reached out and held her father close. "We'll be OK, you and me and Wendy. We'll be OK, Daddy."

Tears moistened the man's face and fell unseen from his cheeks. The soft darkness of the room wrapped the two in silence and hid their sorrow from the glaring lights of the city far below.

* * * * *

"Tyler Hanson, have I got good news for you!" The always jubilant voice of Micky Pratt burst through the open door and bounced off the rows of legal books that lined the company library.

Mr. Hanson glanced up just in time to see a smiling, youthful face follow the sound into the room.

"I could use some good news," the man seated at the long table replied. "Wait, let me guess. You've won the lottery and can now pay back the 500 bucks you owe me."

"Oh, no," the young man laughed. "Much better than that."

"This I've got to hear."

"Well." Micky seated himself across from Mr. Hanson and grinned over at his friend.

"Well . . . what?" the man urged.

Micky looked as if he'd explode with the news he was about to announce. "Tyler Hanson," he said with building excitement, "I've got the perfect woman for you."

The older man closed his eyes and moaned. "Micky. I've told you not to do this. You shouldn't try to set me up with anyone. I'm just not—"

"But she's beautiful!"

Mr. Hanson grimaced. "That's what you said about the last young lady you threw in my lap."

"Well, she *was beautiful.*"

"Micky!" The older man's voice rose in frustration. "She was six feet eight inches tall! I felt like a Munchkin from the Land of Oz standing next to her."

"So?" Micky spread his hands apart. "She plays basketball. Is that so terrible?"

"Not to another basketball player. Besides, she kept patting me on the top of the head. I hate it when women pat me on the top of my head."

"But, you're so cute," the younger man teased. "Besides, how long have we known each other? Ten? Fifteen years?"

"Three. Three long years."

"There, you see? We're buddies, old friends, pals. We have to look out for each other. It's time for you to find some nice female type person and . . . and . . ."

"And what?"

"And get married again. For the kids. You know, Becky and Breezy."

"That's Debbie and Wendy."

"Yeah, them too. They need a mother. You need a wife. It's perfect."

Mr. Hanson stood and gathered up his collection of books. "I appreciate your intense interest in my personal life, but, I'm not ready to find another woman. I've got two sweet little girls looking out for me as it is. That's quite enough for the time being."

"Whatever you say," came the disappointed reply, "but your biographical clock is ticking away. You can't ignore it."

"My *biological* clock is keeping perfect time, thank you very much."

Micky followed Mr. Hanson out of the room and through the office lobby. "I'll tell you what I'll do."

"No."

"I'll have her come up for a short visit."

"*No.*"

"Then you can see what she looks like."

"NO!"

Micky stopped in mock confusion. "Are you saying you don't want to meet this wonderful creature?"

Mr. Hanson rushed into his office and slammed the door. Micky turned and ambled over to Martha's desk. "I think he's warming to the idea," he said.

The phone rang just as the lawyer seated himself behind the morning's pile of mail.

"Hello?"

"Abernathy here," the voice on the line reported. "We've got a problem."

"What is it, Captain? You sound concerned."

"Well, I am. You know that Joey Dugan boy?"

"Yes."

"He's gone."

Mr. Hanson scooted his chair up to his desk and grabbed a pencil. "What do you mean, he's gone?"

"Just what I said. He's gone, escaped, vanished. The guard we posted outside his door went to look in on him early this morning and the bed was empty. We're guessing he got out onto the fire escape and climbed down to the street."

Mr. Hanson ran his fingers through his hair. "That's all he needs. He's in enough trouble as it is."

"Well, that's the other thing I wanted to tell you. Li Fong's daughter finally gave our investigator a description of the man who gunned down her father. She said he was around 40 years old and had a mustache."

"Oh, great," the lawyer groaned. "Joey thinks he's

running from a murder charge. We'll never find him."

The voice on the line paused. "We still have him on a concealed weapon charge. He must have found that gun at the crime scene, just like he said. The real murderer probably tossed it into the gutter, hoping no one would discover it. Along comes sharp-eyed Joey, spots the gun—not knowing a murder had just been committed with it—picks it up, hears the sirens, and runs like a scared dog.

"The police officers think they see a suspect fleeing the crime scene and give chase. The car crashes, Joey stops to help, gets blown through a store window after saving Miller and Gabriel, ends up in the hospital, and gets charged for a murder he didn't know anything about. Not a real good night for the lad."

The lawyer nodded. "I'll say. Do you have people out looking for him?"

"Not really. Since the charge has been downgraded from a felony to a misdemeanor, it's not priority anymore. We'll get around to it when we can."

"But," Mr. Hanson argued, "he thinks he's wanted for murder. He's probably scared to death."

"Listen." The lawyer heard papers being shuffled at the other end of the line. "I can give you his home address. Feel free to check it out. Maybe he'll show up there." Mr. Hanson copied down the information as the captain dictated over the phone. Then the policeman paused. "I'm really sorry about this, Tyler. Keep us informed. Good luck."

Mr. Hanson hung up the phone and leaned back in his chair. His thoughts returned to his conversation with Joey yesterday afternoon at the hospital. He could see the young face, the tubes, the wires, the look in those dark eyes. "I ain't got no system working for me," the boy had said.

It seemed Joey was right. The system had faltered, broken down, and then because of busy schedules and more pressing business, it had vanished all together, leaving a 15-year-old bad boy from the East Side running scared. *How lonely that must feel,* the lawyer thought. *How lonely and hopeless.*

The man rose and walked to the window of his office. He gazed down on the streets far below. People and vehicles moved like multi-colored pebbles across a desert of asphalt. He couldn't see the faces of the people. He didn't know anything about them, only that they were part of the city—the impersonal, uncaring, unseeing city.

How many lives were filled with fear down there? he wondered. *How many eyes searched for love and understanding and couldn't find them in the faces rushing by? How many hearts felt alone, cut off from the warmth of someone, anyone, who would take the time to care?*

Joey Dugan was a victim of the city. The streets held him captive, a prisoner of fear, of mistrust. Yet, he had stopped to save the lives of two people who represented everything he despised, everything he was determined to escape from.

The lawyer let his gaze drift upward until he was looking across the tops of neighboring buildings, across the Hudson River, across the distant towers that lined the Jersey shore, to the horizon. He could see clouds floating in the deep blue ocean of air.

His mind picked up the journey where his eyes had to falter. He saw land stretching wide and green across a rolling expanse of country. From deep in his memory he reconstructed farms bordered by neat rows of fences, hills dotted with cows, roads that ran straight and true, crisscrossing the pastures and croplands like

36

lines drawn with some majestic ruler.

Then the land began to rise—slowly at first, then suddenly, in towering thrusts, sending rock and soil high into the sky. Amid the mountain ranges he saw a little valley where a creek ran free, its waters sparkling in the bright morning sun.

There was a house there, a big house, and on the porch sat two people with smiling faces and hands outstretched in welcome. How beautiful it was. How peaceful. How—

"Mr. Hanson?" Martha's voice shattered the vision, sending it spinning and crashing into the steamy streets far below.

"Mr. Hanson, are you OK?"

The man turned and walked slowly back to his desk. He sat down and buried his face in his hands.

Martha hurried over and placed her hand on her boss's shoulder. "Mr. Hanson, what's wrong? Should I call a doctor?"

The lawyer looked up and smiled. "No, Martha. I'm OK. I just . . ."

"You gave me quite a start there. It was like you didn't know I was here. I called several times."

"Martha?" The lawyer leaned back in his chair. "Have you ever felt like . . . just . . . leaving it all behind?"

"Whatever do you mean?" the woman asked, unsure of what to say.

"I don't know. Sometimes I feel helpless. Things happen I can't control. My daughters need a mother, and I failed to keep one around for them. I guide clients through the legal system and it simply deposits them back on the streets where they can get in trouble all over again. And in the case of Joey Dugan, he's running from something he didn't even do, yet no one has time to run after him and tell him."

The man closed his eyes. "I feel helpless. Totally helpless. I feel like I'm part of a system that doesn't work anymore."

A smile began to spread across Martha's face.

"I don't see anything funny about this," Mr. Hanson said coldly.

The woman leaned forward and looked into the lawyer's eyes. "I'm not laughing at you, Tyler," she said. "It's just that I've heard these same words before, about 15 years ago."

Realization crept into the man's face. "My dad?"

"Yes. He sat right here in this office and made that same speech, and he was just as troubled, just as confused, as you are. He moved away soon after that, leaving some smart-headed, I'm-out-to-change-the-world college graduate in charge. Remember?"

"Was I really that gung-ho?"

"Oh, yeah! You were going to turn New York City on its ear." The woman softened. "And you have, in your own small way. Tyler, you're more like your dad than you think. You two have the same values, the same desire to help people. That's rare in this city. Very rare."

"A whole lot of good it does," the man said with a sigh.

Martha turned to leave, then paused. "You want to change the world, Tyler? Then change a life, just one life. The world will have to adjust."

The office door closed quietly, leaving the man lost in thought. Change a life. Could he do it? He walked back to the window and looked toward the horizon. The clouds had lifted. It seemed he could see much further now.

CHAPTER THREE

DIZZY

★ ★ ★

Jacked-up cars and piles of uncollected rubbish greeted Mr. Hanson as he stepped out of the taxicab. The driver took his money and beat a hasty retreat, leaving the man standing alone, facing rows of battered apartment buildings and graffiti-decorated store fronts.

A dog barked somewhere in the shadows as bits of a newspaper blew across the potholed street.

Faces appeared, then vanished behind darkened windows. The only constant sound to be heard was the distant rumble of traffic on Franklin D. Roosevelt Drive as it skirted the East River, heading north toward Harlem.

The lawyer had the uncomfortable feeling he was being watched, not by a single pair of eyes, but by many. Yet the few pedestrians who passed him took no notice of his existence.

He reached into his pocket and pulled out the small

slip of paper on which he'd scribbled Joey Dugan's home address. Studying the faded numbers on the buildings, he started walking in the direction he felt he should go.

The buildings looked alike, as if they'd all been damaged in the same war. Except, there had been no war in New York's Lower East Side, unless the simple act of living in such a harsh environment could be considered a conflict.

Occasionally a man or woman would brush by. They didn't lift their eyes from the street. They walked like robots, programmed to go about their duties quickly, silently, without awareness of life beyond their own thoughts.

Mr. Hanson moved steadily up the street, reading the numbers above each entrance. Forty-four, 46, 48. Yes. There was apartment building number 48. He crossed the street and climbed the broad, dirty steps. The front door had been snapped off one of its hinges; its cracked and chipped wood protested loudly as he pulled it aside and passed into a small entryway.

The lawyer scanned the rows of buttons and names crowding a panel on the wall. Finding a button labeled "2-B" he pressed it. Somewhere far away he heard a low, muffled buzz.

"Go away." A thick, female voice rattled in the little speaker mounted above the panel.

"Hello?" Mr. Hanson leaned forward. "I'm Tyler Hanson."

"So?"

"I'm looking for Joey Dugan. Is he in?"

"Why do you want to know?"

The man cleared his throat. "I'd like to talk to him, that's all."

There was silence for a moment, then the voice returned. "You a cop?"

"No. I'm a lawyer."

"How nice for you."

Mr. Hanson shook his head. "Look, is Joey home or not?"

"Listen, Mr. Lawyer whoever you are, I don't know and I don't care where that little brat is. I ain't his mother and I ain't his keeper. So go away and bother somebody else."

The speaker clicked as the voice faded. Mr. Hanson stood staring at the number. How could people live like this? How could people turn their backs on family and friends?

"Say, young man?" A small, quiet voice called from just inside the tightly closed door that led into the first floor of the building.

"Yes?"

"Step back a little. I'd like to talk to you."

The lawyer moved back out of the tiny entryway and stood at the top of the stoop. He watched as the door creaked open and an old woman stepped into the light. Her pale face was framed by soft tufts of unruly gray hair. Her eyes, questioning but kind, contrasted with her wrinkled skin. She moved slowly, deliberately, as though she were in pain.

"Arthritis," the woman explained when she saw the man waiting for her. "I get it just before it rains. It's going to rain, you know. Soon."

She hobbled out onto the little porch and lowered her frail, bony body onto a bent and rusted chair. "There we are," the woman said as she adjusted her faded but neatly ironed dress. "I've sat up here every nice day for the last 63 years." She surveyed the street. "A lot has changed. It wasn't always like this."

41

Mr. Hanson leaned against the handrail and studied the old woman. "You know Joey Dugan?"

"Oh, yes. I couldn't help overhearing your conversation with 2-B. I must apologize for the lady who lives there. Not very congenial."

The man smiled. "Not very."

"My name's Pierce, Elizabeth Pierce. You can call me Lizzy."

"OK, Lizzy. What can you tell me about Joey?"

"What's he done now?"

Mr. Hanson looked out onto the street. "It's not so much what he's done as what he thinks he's done."

The old woman spoke softly. "Deep down, he's a good boy, Mr. Hanson. But you already know that or you wouldn't be here."

The man nodded. "I guess you're right."

"You see," Lizzy continued, "Joey tries too hard. And the more he tries, the more he gets himself knocked down. Pretty soon he wants to give up, so I tell him he can't do that, because the neighborhood is filled with people who've just given up. Joey has potential, real potential."

Mr. Hanson sat down on the top step. "Tell me about him, Lizzy. What's he like?"

The old woman smiled a wrinkled smile. "He was such a cute child. He'd come running down the hall as fast as he could and burst into my apartment. 'Dizzy? Dizzy?' he'd shout in his sweet little-boy voice. He called me 'Dizzy' cause his l's weren't too good.

" 'Look, Dizzy,' he'd say, 'I can do a trick. You wanna see?' or 'Look, Dizzy, I can write my name!' or 'Look, Dizzy, I got new shoes.' He has always had such a joy for life. Everything's important. Nothing escapes him. Nothing."

Lizzy paused, then continued, her words filling

with pride. "He says I'm his best friend. Everyday he comes to visit. We talk about things and have cookies and sometimes a little ice cream. He tells me his dreams, about how someday he's going to go far away and live in a place where there are trees and flowers and birds. He loves to dream, Mr. Hanson." Her voice faltered. "He loves to dream."

A shadow crossed the old woman's face. "He came to visit me early this morning. He was hurting. Looked terribly pale. He'd been cut pretty bad. I asked him what happened. He told me everything."

Gazing into the lawyer's eyes she pleaded, "Mr. Hanson, Joey couldn't possibly have killed that man. The boy may lift a loaf of bread from the corner market when he's hungry or help himself to a pair of socks at the store. He may even talk and act tough, but, he's no killer. Not my Joey."

The man nodded. "You're right, Lizzy. He didn't kill anyone. The daughter of the store owner has come forward with a description of the real gunman. Joey's off the hook. But he was carrying a concealed weapon. I've got to find him. Can you help me?"

A deep sigh rattled in the old woman's chest. "I knew he couldn't hurt another human being. I just knew it." Motioning for the lawyer to bend close she whispered, "Go to the big warehouse two blocks east of here. That's where he hides when he's in trouble. Tell him to come home. Tell him his Dizzy wants to see him."

Mr. Hanson smiled. "I'll do that, Lizzy. You can count on it."

The man rose and walked down the steps. At the sidewalk he turned and looked up at the old woman sitting in the bent and rusted chair.

"You've proved me wrong, Lizzy Pierce," he said.

43

"There are still a few left in the city who remember how to love. I was beginning to wonder."

The woman nodded. "Love can grow almost anywhere, young man. You just got to take it out and exercise it every once in a while."

Mr. Hanson waved and began walking. He could see the old, battered warehouse, its windows shattered, its timbers rotting. Even from two blocks away it looked like the perfect place for a frightened boy to hide.

"Joey?" the lawyer called as he reached the large front door that led into the big, abandoned building. His voice echoed along the high walls and long, dirty floor before fading at the far end of the structure.

Mr. Hanson surveyed the immense room as he carefully stepped around piles of empty cardboard boxes and rotting floor tiles. The air was heavy with dust. Brilliant shafts of light, streaming from the broken windows on the south side, pierced the darkness. They illuminated in stark detail the crumbling masonry and long-forgotten machinery. The shafts looked like giant spotlights pinpointing actors in a play. But here on this stage of ruin, nothing moved.

"Joey? Can you hear me?"

The man looked for recent tracks in the dusty floor. Over by one of the walls something caught his eye. Moving in that direction he stooped and ran his fingers through a puddle of bright-red liquid. It was blood.

"Joey!" he called again, this time his voice strained, fearful.

At the far end of the building something clattered to the floor. Looking up, the man saw a form staggering along an elevated walkway just under the windows.

"Joey, stop," the lawyer called out. "You're hurt. I want to help you."

The form hesitated, framed by the bright light streaming through a large opening behind it.

"Please, Joey. You don't have to run." Mr. Hanson edged toward the silhouetted outline. "I've got to talk to you."

A weak, young voice spoke from the walkway. "Yeah, sure. You want to catch me so you can—" A deep cough wrenched itself from the boy's throat. "—so you can send me to jail. No way, man. I didn't do nothing. I swear it."

"Joey, listen. I—"

"No, you listen, mister high and mighty lawyer. Why should I trust you? You're no different than everybody else. First you say you wanna help, then when the chips are down you'll disappear, just like all the rest. Nobody stays around. They just leave. Nobody cares about what happens to a guy like me. I'm left holding the bag like some kinda stupid fool."

The lawyer stood looking up at the form in front of the window. "What about Lizzy Pierce, Joey? She hasn't given up on you."

Mr. Hanson saw the boy reach up and cover his face with his hands. Sobs echoed from deep inside the young chest. "She's different," he whispered.

"That's right, Joey. She loves you," the man said. "That's why she's different. Love does that to people. It makes them stay right beside you when everyone else runs away. It gives you someplace to go when you're hurting. But you have to let people love you. Not everyone will, but chances are you'll find someone who's willing to. Someone like Lizzy."

The form on the walkway swayed from side to side. The boy reached down to steady himself on the wooden handrail. Mr. Hanson knew the teenager was weakening from loss of blood.

"Listen, Joey," the lawyer urged, trying to position himself nearer the teetering form. "Give me a chance to prove to you I won't leave you, either. Just give me one chance. That's all I ask. OK, Joey? I won't let you down."

He listened for an answer. A weak voice drifted in the still, dusty air. "You promise?"

Tears stung the lawyer's eyes. "Yeah, Joey. I promise."

The boy's legs buckled. He leaned forward onto the handrail. Mr. Hanson heard a snap as the rotten wood gave way, sending the small body out into space. Joey fell, turning slowly through the air before crashing into a pile of boxes resting on the warehouse floor.

The lawyer quickly pawed his way to the center of the pile, lifting moldy boxes and tossing them aside. In moments he was kneeling beside the still, ashen form.

"Oh, Lord," he prayed, "don't let him die here. Please, don't let him die."

"Help!" the lawyer shouted, his call echoing through the vast, empty warehouse. "Help us!"

Realizing no one could hear, he raced across the deserted room and stumbled out of the building. Running down the street he cried, "Somebody call an ambulance!" His voice shook with fear. "Please, somebody help!"

No one moved. Doors and windows remained tightly shut. Store owners stared from their doorways or simply turned their backs and walked into the shadows.

"What's wrong with you?" the man screamed. "There's a hurt boy in the warehouse. He needs help right now!"

People went about their business, ignoring the man in the street.

Racing to a grocery store, Mr. Hanson entered and looked around wildly. "Phone!" he shouted to the man behind the cash register. "Where's your phone?"

The man motioned toward the rear of the store. The lawyer sped down the aisle, almost toppling a couple of shoppers who stood in his way.

Grabbing the receiver, he frantically dialed 911. "Help me," he shouted into the handset as a distant voice answered. "My name is Tyler Hanson and we have a badly hurt boy in the warehouse on 9th Street just east of Tompkins Square Park. Hurry. Please! He may be dying."

Slamming the phone back on its hook, the man turned and raced out of the store, across the street, and up into the big warehouse. Breathlessly he knelt beside the young boy lying at the center of the scattered pile of boxes. Cradling the teenager in his arms, he rocked back and forth in the stillness.

"Joey," the lawyer said softly, his voice choked with tears, "you're innocent. Can you hear me? You're innocent. You didn't hurt anybody. It was a mistake."

Looking down into the ashen face nestled in his arms, the man seemed to be gazing at all the hurt, all the hopelessness, all the sorrow that lives in every street, in every city. "Oh, Joey," he moaned, "don't die. Please don't die. You have to know there are people who love you. You have to know I love you."

Holding the boy in his arms, the man wept openly, unconstrained. The wide, empty warehouse echoed his sobs. Far in the distance a siren's wail cut through the heavy air as the city went about its business. There was much to do, and so little time.

CHAPTER FOUR

AWAKENING

★ ★ ★

Rain fell steadily, softly, sending tiny liquid rivers coursing aimlessly down the panes of glass that separated the small hospital room from the damp air outside.

Occasionally far-off lightning would blink, illuminating in faint silver light the early morning darkness of the room.

In the shadows slept a boy, his bruised and battered body wrapped in healing bonds of white gauze. Nearby a stand held a plastic bag of plasma. The life-giving fluid slipped down a long flexible tube and entered the outstretched arm resting on the bed.

Two days had passed since the scene at the warehouse. But the teenager would not remember what happened during that time. He did not feel the gentle hands that lifted him from the pile of cardboard boxes and bore his unconscious form to the waiting ambulance. He would not recall the speeding journey to the hospital, the nurses and doctors who worked tirelessly to close his wounds, to revitalize his fading heartbeat, to save his life.

Joey Dugan would not realize that all through his surgery, his hours in the recovery room, and the jolting gurney ride to the third floor there had been someone at his side. Even now that someone sat across the room, fitfully sleeping in a hard, wooden chair.

Had he been conscious, Joey would have seen the concerned eyes of the lawyer watching, as hour after hour, medications worked in concert with nature to bring healing to his exhausted, hurting body.

He would have heard the nurses speaking softly, encouragingly, to him. And just yesterday, he would have felt the presence of Captain Abernathy as he stood by his bed and talked to the lawyer.

"I'm sorry, Tyler," the policeman had said. "I had no idea how serious all this was. He was hurt bad by the explosion, wasn't he?"

"Running away didn't help any, either," Mr. Hanson had replied. "He was so scared. And it was all our fault. We took unconfirmed evidence and pronounced him guilty. I don't blame him for running. I would've, too. But he had no place to go. There was no one to shelter him. Lizzy Pierce did what she could, but he didn't want her to get into trouble because of him. That's why he went to the warehouse. He was so alone up there on the walkway. So frightened."

The older man had placed his arm around his friend. "Tyler," he'd said, "I can see Joey Dugan is no criminal, at least, not a dangerous one. We're dropping the weapons charge. We have the gun. It's off the streets. That's what's important."

Before leaving, Captain Abernathy had paused at the door. "When Joey gets better, bring him by the station. We've got a couple of men who'd like to say thank you." Glancing at the still form lying on the bed, the captain had added, "And there's another man there who'd like to say he's sorry."

Joey had heard none of this. Now, as dawn began to glow across the cloud-painted eastern sky, he stirred.

It seemed to the boy as if he were emerging from a dark, endless tunnel. Sounds were muffled, soft, barely discernible. A tiny, faint pin-prick of light floated far ahead. He moved effortlessly toward it. His breathing became deeper as his lungs expanded, taking in more and more air.

The light drifted closer, slowly at first, then faster and faster. He could feel his heart rate quicken. His arms and legs began to tingle as his blood pressure increased. He could hear himself breathing.

A low moan rose in his chest as he watched the light rush toward him. Then, in a blinding flash, he was awake, sitting up in bed, screaming.

Mr. Hanson, jolted by the sound, almost tumbled from his chair. He looked up to see the boy fall back against his pillow, the young chest heaving, gasping for air.

The boy screamed again, then was silent. The lawyer rushed to his side. "Joey! Joey! It's OK. I'm here. Look at me. I'm right here!"

Joey's eyelids fluttered, then opened slowly. A face drifted in and out of focus above him. He could hear a man's voice calling his name. He fought to stay conscious. The voice sounded kind, concerned, urgent.

"Joey," the voice repeated over and over again, "fight it. Come on, Joey. Fight to stay awake!"

There was something strangely familiar about the sound of the voice. Where had he heard it before? Wait. Yes. The warehouse. He'd heard it at the warehouse.

He was standing up on the walkway and the voice was calling to him from below. That was it. The walkway. The railing. No! It's breaking away. The railing is breaking. Falling. Falling!

Joey reached up and grabbed Mr. Hanson around the neck. He held tightly until the vision faded. Then he sank back against his pillow. The face came into sharp focus. It was the lawyer from the warehouse. What was he doing here? Wait. Where's here?

The boy looked around the room. What was this place?

"Joey," the man was saying quietly, "you're in the hospital. You've been asleep for two days, but now you're going to be fine. Do you understand?"

The teenager shook his head slowly. "Hospital?" he repeated. "I'm in the hospital?"

"That's right. And I'm here with you. You're not alone. You don't have to be alone anymore."

Joey looked up into the kind, unshaven face hovering above him. Yes. He remembered now. It was all coming back.

"You . . ." the boy said, his voice not much above a whisper, ". . . you did stay with me. You didn't leave."

"No, I didn't. I promised, remember?"

The teenager's swollen and bruised face brightened with a hint of a smile. "Yeah, I remember. I remember everything."

Mr. Hanson placed his hand on the boy's shoulder. "I'm going to call the doctor, Joey. He said to let him know when you came around. You gave us all quite a scare. Welcome back."

The teenager closed his eyes and sighed a long, happy sigh. "You . . . stayed with me." His words, though faltering, were filled with wonder. "You actually . . . stayed with me. You're a friend, a real friend.

I ain't . . . had . . . too many of those. Just Lizzy. And now you too. I'm a . . . a lucky guy."

"Yeah, Joey," the man said, brushing a tear from his cheek. "It's about time someone brought a little luck into your life."

The boy lifted his hand and touched Mr. Hanson's arm. "For a hotshot . . . lawyer, you ain't so bad."

Mr. Hanson smiled, then headed for the door. "Don't go anywhere. I'll be right back." Suddenly he stopped in his tracks. "And, hey, Joey, have I got some news for you! I'm talking good news. Better than you've ever heard before. I'll tell you when I get back."

Joey waved weakly. "Mr. Hanson?" he said.

"Yes?"

"See if you can find . . . a . . . pizza somewhere. I'm . . . starving."

The lawyer closed his eyes and breathed a silent prayer. "Thank You, God," he said. "Thank You for Joey."

In the hallway he turned and headed for the nurses' station. "Excuse me, ma'am," he called excitedly to the woman sitting behind the long, white desk. "How about ordering us a pizza. We've got a hungry boy in here!"

* * * * *

Debbie blinked and tried not to cry. The man on the television screen was telling his dearest, fondest, most favorite girl that he was leaving. "Heading west where a man can see the stars," he said.

The girl in the red and yellow bonnet dabbed her eyes with her handkerchief. "I understand, Jeb," she said, lifting her hand gracefully in the air. "You gotta fly like the eagles. I mustn't hold you down."

With those words ringing in his ears, the man mounted his trusty horse and rode toward the setting sun. "Remember me," he called mournfully. "When you hear a coyote's howl or a prairie dog's yelp, think of me."

The woman fluttered to the ground in sorrow. "I will, Jeb, I will."

With a final flourish and a cloud of dust, the man and horse crested the top of the hill and were gone.

Orchestra music rose to a crescendo and then the picture faded to black. Debbie clicked off the set with the remote control and stood looking toward the window. "You gotta fly like the eagles," she wailed. "I mustn't hold you down."

"Then don't." Wendy entered the room and headed for the kitchen.

"Ah, what do you know about true romance?" the older girl chided. "Someday a big, handsome cowboy will come and sweep me off my feet." The girl whirled about the living room. "We'll ride off into the sunset together. It will be so romantic."

Wendy rolled her eyes. "When I get older, am I going to be a total loony like you?"

Debbie scowled. "Romance is serious stuff. It's the song of the heart."

"Forget the heart," Wendy shot back. "My stomach is singing a pretty loud song right now. What's for supper?"

The older girl swirled and pranced to the refrigerator. She flung open the door with a graceful brush of her hand and stood staring into its cold depths. "We've got yogurt. We've got yesterday's casserole. We've got something in a plastic bag that looks like it used to be some sort of food, and we have a nutritious tossed salad."

Wendy joined her sister at the refrigerator door. "And," she announced pointing toward the freezer section, "we have ice cream."

"YES!" Debbie cried. "The perfect food. Little sister, this is the only thing we agree on. We both love strawberry ice cream."

"Chocolate," Wendy countered.

"You get the spoons. I'll get the bowls. We'll live a little."

With happy squeals, the girls dished heaping piles of the frozen treat into large cereal bowls and sat down cross-legged on the kitchen floor to enjoy their rather singular supper.

"You know," Wendy said between mouthfuls, "I think it's neat Daddy's helping that boy at the hospital. I mean, the poor guy thought he was wanted for murder! Wow. If I knew the cops were chasing me for something I didn't do, I'd run like crazy, too."

"Yeah. You'd run to this apartment and they'd come up and arrest me for harboring a fugitive."

Wendy thought for a moment, then asked, "Have you noticed anything strange about Daddy during the past few weeks? Ever since his little rendezvous at the warehouse, he's been acting mighty weird."

Debbie savored another spoonful of strawberry ice cream. "You mean like those late-night phone calls to Grandpa?"

"Yeah. They talk for hours. I overheard him the other night when I got up to go to the bathroom. Daddy was talking about getting a new partner for his business or something like that. I couldn't hear too good."

The older girl raised her eyebrows. "And have you seen those big boxes that cute guy from Parcel Express brought up? What muscles!"

"The boxes had muscles?"

"No, stupid, the cute guy had muscles. The boxes had computer stuff in them. One had 'Horizon PC' written on it. The other was labeled 'Quick-Link Fax.' Then there were some marked with software names I've heard him mention in the past. He's buying the latest computer equipment like there's no tomorrow."

Debbie scratched her head thoughtfully. "What's going on? Daddy's being very mysterious."

"And he's smiling all the time, like he knows some secret he's not telling us. It's spooky."

About that time the front door opened and Mr. Hanson entered, his arms filled with odd-shaped packages. Seeing the two girls sitting on the kitchen floor, he called out, "Howdy, my little wranglers. I see you're having chow. Well, let me bed down my horse and I'll join you there by the ol' campfire."

The girls stared at each other. "This is getting weirder and weirder," Debbie whispered.

The man dropped his packages on the sofa. "First, my little cowpokes, I have something for you. Saunter on over here and take a gander."

Debbie and Wendy set their bowls of ice cream on the counter, then shyly moved in the direction of the strange man who looked very much like their father.

Reaching into a big box, the stranger lifted out a large, white western hat and placed it on his head. He looked first at one girl, then the other.

"So? What do you think?"

Debbie stifled a laugh. "You look like Hopalong Lawyer. Been herding taxicabs, Daddy?"

"I know what you're thinking," the man said, reaching into the same bag.

"I doubt that," Debbie mumbled to her sister.

Ignoring the comment, the man continued. "You're saying to yourself, 'Boy, I wish I had a swell hat like that.' Well, here you are. Wish no more." Two additional white, but smaller, hats emerged from the shopping bag.

The girls gingerly took the headgear from their father's outstretched hands. They slowly placed the wide-brimmed hats on their heads and looked at each other.

"Don't you look terrific," the man beamed. "And you thought I didn't know fashion. Ha!"

"What's in the other boxes, Daddy?" Debbie said hesitatingly, afraid of what she might hear.

· "Just look at this!" the man said triumphantly as he started pulling articles of clothing from the collection of boxes piled on the sofa. "We've got western shirts and western slacks and big, wide western belts. And here's a pair of chaps." He paused for emphasis. "Everyone needs a good pair of chaps."

Wendy's eyes grew bigger and bigger as each new piece of clothing came from the boxes. "I get it! I get it!" she cried. "We're all going to join a circus."

"Nope."

"We're preparing for Halloween early?" Debbie encouraged.

"Nope."

The man flopped down on the sofa amid the piles of clothes. "Girls, I want to talk to you."

The two sisters sat down on the thickly carpeted floor at their father's feet.

"I've been doing a lot of thinking lately," he began, a seriousness creeping into his voice. "Sometimes a man gets so involved with life that he forgets what's really important, what really matters. You may have noticed I've been acting a little strange lately."

"Oh," Debbie said, eyeing the scattered piles of western ware, "have you really?"

The man smiled. "Well, there's a reason for all this.

Call it mid-life crisis, call it burnout, call it whatever you like, but I have to make a change. A big change."

Mr. Hanson sighed. "I guess my experience with Joey Dugan has forced me to reexamine my life. I've come to realize that there's more to living than making a bunch of money. I represent wealthy people all the time, and most of them aren't truly happy. The only ones who are, use their fortunes to help other people. That's what I want to do. I want to help people."

The room was quiet for a long moment. "I've been talking with my father. Actually, he's been talking to me for years, trying to get me to do something, but I've been holding out. Well, no longer. I'm going to give it a try."

Debbie studied the man's face. "What are you going to do, Daddy?"

"*I'm* not going to do it," he said with a smile. "*We're* going to do it."

Wendy edged up to her father's knee. "Well?" she urged.

Mr. Hanson looked at one girl, then the other. He drew in a deep breath. "We're going to move to Montana," he announced.

The sisters sat in stunned silence as their father spoke with growing excitement. "I realize you two have never been there. I've only visited the ranch where your grandparents live one time, back when Debbie was 2 and Wendy hadn't even been thought of. As you may remember, your mother refused to travel anywhere west of Trenton, New Jersey, so the only contact I've had with my parents has been by phone and the three times they came here to visit us during Christmas holidays. Remember?"

The girls nodded slowly.

"Well, Dad and I have a plan. I'm going to run a

home office from the ranch. I've purchased some powerful computer equipment so I can access my New York firm and some of the country's largest legal data bases. I'll do research for my clients while my new partners represent them in court. At the same time, we'll be preparing a very special project I'm not going to tell you about because we're still working on it. You'll find out soon enough."

The man closed his eyes. "We'll be out of the city, away from the pressures, away from all the hurt, out where I can raise my girls surrounded by the beauty of nature and the songs of birds. Grandpa says he's excited about this." Mr. Hanson looked lovingly at his two daughters. "I want you to be excited, too."

Wendy sat looking at the floor. The man noticed a tear slip from her eye and move down her soft cheek.

"Wendy," Mr. Hanson said softly, "why are you crying? Don't you want to live in a beautiful valley with Grandpa and Grandma?"

The girl sobbed quietly.

"Honey, what's wrong?"

Wendy looked up into her father's face. "How will Mother find us?"

The man lifted his youngest daughter into his lap. "Oh, sweetheart," he said, holding her close. "Oh, my precious little girl. Look, I'll tell you what we'll do. I'll give you a map showing right where the ranch is, and you can send it to her. You can give her the phone number, the address, and even what airplanes fly out that way." Mr. Hanson glanced at Debbie and continued. "Then, if she wants, she can come out to see us. How's that sound?"

The younger girl wiped her face and looked up into the eyes of her father. "I guess that would be OK," she said. "Can I have a horse?"

The man laughed. "Grandpa has one picked out for you already. Says his name is Early."

"Early?" Wendy asked.

"Grandpa says he was born first in the season, always eats ahead of the other horses, gets up before the sun comes up, and is the first horse he's ever seen that goes to bed before all the others. So they named him Early."

"What color is he?"

"Brown, with a white star between his eyes. Grandpa says he may turn more reddish, but it's too early to tell."

Wendy giggled. "Wow. My very own horse." She picked up her new hat and placed it on her head. "Hey, Early," she called. "It's roundup time."

The youngster slipped from her father's knee and skipped across the room. "Faster, Early, faster," she coaxed the imaginary horse below her. "Let's go hunt a grizzly."

Mr. Hanson shook his head and smiled. "That horse will never be the same." Glancing down at Debbie, his smile faded.

"You don't like the idea, do you?"

The older girl stared at the hat resting in her lap. "If it were just an idea, it'd be OK. But you never even talked to me about it. You never even mentioned it. Didn't you think I'd like to be involved in the decision-making process?"

"I'm sorry, Debbie," the man said. "You're right. But can't you see? This is important to me."

"Well, there are things important to me too," the girl countered angrily. "What about my friends here in New York? And my school? Don't these count? You just went ahead and made decisions and didn't even bother to talk to me about it."

Mr. Hanson nodded. "You're right. I forgot that you're not a little girl anymore, that you have a life of your own to live. But it's my job to take care of you and Wendy. Montana just seems like a way of protecting my two little—uh, my one little girl and my other growing-up lady, from all the bad I see here in the city."

"I don't see anything so awful here," Debbie announced coldly.

"I believe you," the man said quietly. "Maybe that's the problem. Maybe you should be seeing it, maybe you should be noticing the greed and dishonesty that surrounds life in the big city like a muzzle. Love has been replaced with mistrust. People who want to care about others find it very hard to do so."

"You think running off to Montana is going to solve everything?"

The man was silent for a moment. "No, but it will certainly be a step in the right direction. I want my girls to learn how to love other people freely, without fear. I want you to breathe air that hasn't just passed through a bus's tailpipe."

Mr. Hanson reached out and touched his daughter's cheek. "And most of all, I want my sweet Wendy and beautiful Debbie to learn how to love others, to care what happens to the people who pass through their lives. We only have one life to live. I don't want us to miss out on all the happiness that might be waiting for us."

"Daddy," Debbie said, resting her chin on her father's knee, "what if I don't like living in Montana?"

"I'll make a deal with you," the man encouraged. "Give it one year. Just one year. And if you can't stand it, you can come back to New York and attend that fancy boarding school you've told me about—you know, the one guaranteed to make 'women of distinction' out of their pupils."

The girl thought for a moment, then nodded slowly. Smiling up at her father she said, "One year. I guess I can put up with tigers and bears for that long."

"They don't have tigers in Montana," the man laughed. "But bears they've got. Big ones."

Mr. Hanson lifted his hands high in the air and growled fiercely. Debbie screamed in playful terror and hurried across the room, her father in hot pursuit. Wendy rode in from the bedroom and the three chased each other around and around until they dropped in a laughing, gasping heap in the middle of the floor.

The man held his daughters close and smiled a broad, happy smile. At long last, he felt free from the deep worry that had plagued him for years. He was going to take his family out of the city to a land where hopes and dreams can run as free as the clear mountain streams. His precious little girls would learn their lessons from nature, not from the corner magazine stand. Sure, there were many details to be ironed out, but he and Grandpa would find solutions. How good it felt, how very exciting to experience hope again after years of self-doubt and concern.

In the midst of the gaiety he motioned for Debbie and Wendy to listen. "Oh, I forgot to tell you," he said, panting for breath. "We're taking Joey Dugan with us."

CHAPTER FIVE

THE ESCAPE

★ ★ ★

Martha stood shaking her head, a broad smile brightening her face. "I knew it. I just knew it! It was only a matter of time."

Mr. Hanson leaned back in his office chair. "It's not like I'm deserting the fort," he encouraged. "I'm just opening a branch office a thousand or so miles away."

The man motioned toward the newly installed computer terminal resting on a table at one corner of the room. "I'll be in contact with you every single day. You're not going to get rid of me that easy."

The woman eyed the sleek, modern machine with obvious apprehension. "So I'm suppose to learn how to use one of those contraptions?"

The lawyer looked hurt. "That's not a contraption. You're gazing at a turbo-speed electronic wonder with mega-memory and storage capacity enough to fill this office four times with paper documents. That's where you and I will meet everyday. We'll chat, compare notes, exchange gossip, just like we do now."

"Well, I don't know," the woman hesitated. "It's a far cry from simple typing."

Mr. Hanson shrugged. "Think of it as a typewriter with an attitude."

The two laughed out loud. Martha smiled warmly at her boss. "I'm going to miss you, Tyler Hanson, just like I missed your dad when he wised up and finally left this crazy city."

"I'll miss you, too," the man responded. "But you, more than anyone, know why I'm leaving."

"Yeah, I know," Martha conceded. "But it doesn't make it any easier. First your father, then you. Like I said, you two are very much alike."

Mr. Hanson stood and started stuffing papers into his briefcase. "There was a time when I'd take offense at a statement like that. Funny. The older I get, the smarter *he* gets. Kinda scary, if you ask me."

With a wave the man hurried from his office. "I'll be back after lunch," he called over his shoulder. "I'm taking the girls to visit Joey. They've never met him. I'll be at the hospital for about an hour. This should be interesting."

Martha nodded. "Good luck," she said.

Debbie and Wendy were waiting in the hospital lobby when Mr. Hanson's taxi stopped at the curb. He joined his daughters and they all headed for the elevators.

"Now, remember, you two," the man prompted, "Joey is not your normal, everyday individual. He's a street kid who likes to act tough. But deep down, he's just a 15-year-old boy who needs to be loved like everybody else. Think you can handle it?"

Debbie shrugged. "No problem, Daddy. He won't get by with anything as long as I'm around."

The man glanced down at his oldest daughter. "Take it easy on him," he pleaded. "He's only human."

Debbie laughed. "How bad can he be?"

The elevator door slid open, revealing a chaotic frenzy of running nurses and orderlies accompanied by a ringing alarm. Confusion and smoke filled the hallway.

"What's going on here?" Mr. Hanson called to a nurse who was hurrying by, carrying a bedpan brimming with water.

"Someone started a fire, and you'll never guess who," an orderly responded, almost tripping over another man running with a mop bucket.

The smoke seemed to be coming from a room about two thirds of the way down the long hallway. Mr. Hanson recognized whose room it was even before he got to it.

Elbowing his way through the crowd of excited hospital personnel, he entered the small ward. Through the smoke and commotion he saw a lean, brown-haired boy sitting cross-legged on a bed, watching the action and cheering the fire fighters along. Mr. Hanson groaned. The boy on the bed was no other than Joey Dugan.

"Hey, Mr. H," the teenager called. "Some party, eh? Thought I'd liven up the place a bit."

The man grabbed a bucket someone was carrying and hurled the water high into the air. The swirl of liquid passed over the burning bed, over the orderlies pounding the flames with blankets, and squarely onto Joey.

"Hey!" the boy screeched, gasping from the shock of the cold water. "You did that on purpose!"

"Joey Dugan," Mr. Hanson said, moving menacingly toward the young patient, "what are you, *crazy?*

This is a hospital. There are sick people here. Whatever made you set your bed on fire?"

"I got bored," the boy whined, his fine-featured face drooping into a pout. "I wanted a little action. I didn't hurt nobody."

A mighty whooshing sound interrupted the conversation as a bare-armed, burly maintenance woman entered the room brandishing a large fire extinguisher. White foam enveloped the bed and choked out the fire within seconds. Heavy smoke hung in the tension-filled air like storm-clouds over a city.

Mr. Hanson stared at the boy through narrowed eyes. He spoke through tightly pinched lips, his words arriving in short, clipped phrases: "Joey Dugan . . . don't you ever . . . ever . . . pull something like this . . . again. You understand me? Do you?"

The boy blinked.

The lawyer continued. "You have got to start thinking about other people more than yourself. You got bored so you started a fire? Oh that's beautiful, just beautiful." Mr. Hanson motioned toward the group of hospital employees working to clean up the destroyed ward. "Look at these people. They weren't bored, Joey. They were working hard taking care of sick people. But they had to drop everything, they had to leave patients who really needed their help, and come up here to entertain poor, little Joey Dugan by putting out the fire he started.

"That was the most selfish trick I've ever seen anyone pull. I can't believe it. I just can't believe it!"

The man turned and stormed out into the hallway. Debbie and Wendy ran to meet him. "What happened, Daddy? Is Joey OK?"

"Oh, he's fine," Mr. Hanson snapped. "Never better." The lawyer shook his head. "I may have made a mistake, girls. Montana wouldn't be safe with Joey Dugan around. He may get bored and burn the whole state down."

The elevator door opened and an old woman emerged with the crowd of maintenance workers who poured from the cab and flowed down the hallway carrying mops, buckets, and trash bags. She watched them enter the room where curls of white smoke still wafted through the doorway. She saw Mr. Hanson and his two daughters standing over by the nurses' station.

Catching the man's eye, she pointed in the direction of the smoking room. "Joey?" she asked.

Mr. Hanson smiled weakly and hurried over to her. "Lizzy. How nice to see you again. Yeah. That's all Joey's doing. Got bored, he says."

Lizzy closed her eyes and sighed. "I'm sorry. Sometimes he can be rather unthinking."

Mr. Hanson nodded. "I'm not sure how to handle that kind of irresponsibility." He brightened. "Oh, Lizzy, may I present my two daughters, Debbie and Wendy."

"Hi, girls," the woman said extending her hand in greeting. "How lovely you both are. I'm pleased to meet you."

Wendy looked up into the kind face of the visitor. "You know Joey Dugan?"

"We're old friends," Lizzy said, smiling.

Debbie reached out her hand and took Lizzy's in a gentle yet firm grip. "We were about to meet him, but the fire kinda stopped us." Turning to her father she added, "Can we go in now?"

Mr. Hanson sighed. "I don't know, girls. This stunt he just pulled has me concerned. I may not want you to get involved with him."

Wendy looked down the hallway, then back at her

father. "You mean, we're not going to take him to—"

"Wendy," the man interrupted, "let me think a little bit more about that, OK?"

The girl seemed disappointed. Lizzy studied the man's face for a long moment, then she motioned for him to follow her. They strolled down the hallway away from the smoking room.

"Where were you going to take Joey?" she asked when they were far enough from the two girls that their conversation couldn't be overheard.

Mr. Hanson spread his arms in frustration. "It was a silly idea," he said.

Lizzy stopped and touched the man's sleeve. "Mr. Hanson, where were you going to take him?"

The lawyer shook his head from side to side. "My folks have a ranch out west, in Montana. I'm moving out with the girls and thought I'd invite Joey to come along. My father said he could work to earn his keep. I don't know. My dad and I have this big plan of fixing up the place as a summer camp for city kids, but now, after this, I'm not too sure."

Mr. Hanson saw a tear slip slowly down the woman's wrinkled cheek. She looked up into his eyes, her face filled with pleading. "Mr. Hanson. I've never begged anyone for anything in all my life. But I'm about to change that. Please, oh please, take Joey with you. There's nothing for him here in New York. You've seen where he lives. You've seen the streets, the people, the pain. That's what's waiting for Joey Dugan."

She took hold of the man's hand. "You can change all that. You can help him escape a future that's dark and hopeless. Please, Mr. Hanson. God has given you a wonderful plan, not only for Joey but for many others just like him. Please, I beg you, reconsider. Please."

The man hesitated, touched by the woman's concern. "Lizzy, I don't know if I can handle that kind of rebellion. I've got two daughters to think about. I don't want to place them in any kind of danger."

Lizzy nodded. "I understand your apprehension," she admitted softly. "But let me assure you, Joey means no harm. He just doesn't think things through. Don't forget, he hasn't had a father or mother to teach him how to live, how to act. I do the best I can, but I'm just the old woman who lives next door. I'm not with him all the time. He needs someone who can guide him, teach him, love him full-time. He's never had that. Never."

The lawyer ran his fingers through his hair. "Am I being over confident to think I can provide what Joey and kids like him need?"

"I'll tell you the secret of handling street kids," the old woman said. "Don't stop loving them after they do something stupid. Just clean up the mess and love them some more. You may have to repeat the process again and again, but, like water flowing over a stone, you'll wear them down.

"And under all that rough, cutting surface, you'll find children who are simply scared to death that no one loves them. Stay with it. And someday, they'll learn how to communicate their call for help without setting their beds on fire."

Mr. Hanson stood for a long moment, reflecting on what the old woman had said. Finally he turned and looked into her kind blue eyes. "Does the city ever frighten you, Lizzy Pierce? Does anything?"

The woman smiled. "Only when people turn their backs on other people. That scares the daylights out of me."

A smile began to tug at the corners of Mr. Hanson's

mouth. He reached out and drew the old woman into his arms. "God help me," he said. "There must be a conspiracy going on around here. You, my secretary, my dad, even my daughters take pleasure lately in forcing me to do what I think I should do."

"Well, Mr. Hanson," the woman laughed, "you may as well give in. You're outnumbered."

"Please call me Tyler," the lawyer said. "You know me better than I do, so we may as well cut the formality."

"OK, Tyler," Lizzy encouraged. "Now, wasn't there something you came here to do?"

"You sound like my mother," the man said in a pretended whine.

"Good," Lizzy giggled. "I'll take that as a compliment."

The two walked back down the hallway arm in arm toward the smoke-darkened room. Debbie and Wendy were nowhere in sight.

When they reached the entrance to the ward, Mr. Hanson and Lizzy saw Joey sitting on a bed between a couple of visitors. One was in the middle of an exciting story.

"Then, all of a sudden, Grandpa saw a huge, I mean *huge,* mountain lion walking up along the crest of the hill. Well, I don't have to tell you he was a little scared."

"Grandpa or the mountain lion?" Joey asked.

"Grandpa, of course, silly," Wendy said, rolling her eyes. "I mean, wouldn't you be scared, too?"

"Nah," the boy boasted. "I'd just go up there and beat him up."

"Oh, brother," the younger girl moaned. "You don't just beat up a mountain lion!"

"What's going on here?" Mr. Hanson called from

the doorway. "Joey, I see you've met my two daughters."

"Yeah," the boy said, slipping off the bed and picking his way around piles of burnt bed linen. "They were telling me about some ranch somewhere. Hey, Dizzy. You should hear this stuff."

The man eyed his daughters sternly. "You mean my folks' place in Montana?"

"Yeah, Montana," Joey said. Then he hesitated. "Where's this Montana? Out in Long Island?"

The room exploded with laughter. Joey looked at each face with growing frustration. "Hey," he yelled, "what do I know from Montana? Like I'm a world traveler, right?"

Mr. Hanson walked over to the boy and placed his arm around his shoulder. "I'll tell you what, Joey. How would you like to see Montana close up?"

"What, you got a book or something?"

"Better than that," the lawyer said. "We'd like to take you there when we go in a few weeks. You can live on the farm and work for your keep. Of course, maybe you'd rather stay on the Lower East Side and hunt mountain lions along the Hudson River."

The boy stood in stunned silence. He glanced at Lizzy. The old woman smiled and nodded gently. Her eyes shown with happiness.

"Hey, no kidding?" Joey asked, trying to remain calm. "You want to take me to this Montana place?"

"Yeah, no kidding," Mr. Hanson responded in his best New York City drawl. "You can be some kinda city cowboy and ride a horse and hunt grizzly bears before breakfast."

Joey's mouth dropped open. "You ain't kidding, are you? Hey, Dizzy. I'm leaving the city. I'm gettin' out of here. Unbelievable!"

Debbie stood and walked up beside the boy. "Listen, Mr. Dugan," she said in a firm, motherly tone. "You'll have to work hard. Montana is no place for laziness and you can't set any more beds on fire. I'm older than you so you're going to have to do what I tell you. Understand?"

Joey looked at the girl and then at Mr. Hanson. "Does she have to go too?"

The man laughed. "I'm afraid so, Joey. And you'd better do what she says. I think there's mountain lion in her."

The boy glanced back at Debbie. "First I get to leave New York, then I get an older sister. I think this Montana thing is going to be a mixed blessing."

Debbie smiled. "Older sister. Hey, I like the sound of that."

Joey groaned. "That don't surprise me."

Lizzy walked over and wrapped her arms around the boy. "Oh, my little Joey," she said softly. "I'll miss you so much." She placed his young face between her hands and gazed into his eyes. "This is your big chance, Joey. Don't blow it. Make me proud of you."

"Dizzy," the boy said quietly, "you will always be my best friend. Always."

The woman held Joey close. Glancing over at Mr. Hanson, she whispered words only he could hear. "Thank you, Tyler," she said. "Thank you."

* * * * *

The weeks sped by as busy hands sorted and packed, carried and wrapped, boxed and loaded, all the belongings in the Hanson household. Debbie and Wendy worked from dawn till dusk, transforming their comfortable, well-appointed apartment home into an empty shell where only memories lived. The walls stood stark and naked, stripped of picture frames and knick-knacks.

Mr. Hanson spent his days and some of his evenings working closely with his new business partners, bringing them up to date on the company client list, explaining in great detail the needs of each individual who trusted the firm of Hanson & Hanson for legal assistance.

He also took plenty of time to train the unsure Martha how to operate the powerful and super-fast computer system he'd installed.

"Now, Martha," he said one evening after everyone else had gone, "if you ever get confused as to what to do, just push this key marked F10 and a help screen will flash up on the monitor telling you what to do next. Understand?"

Martha studied the keyboard, then the screen. "What do I push when I want to say 'Give me my old typewriter back'?"

Mr. Hanson laughed. "Computers don't have a key for that. It would be considered treason."

The woman sighed. "I figure I may as well learn this stuff. You probably have guessed that me and high technology don't mix too well."

"You'll learn," the lawyer encouraged. "There's no one else in all of New York City who knows this business better than you. We need you very much."

"OK, OK, I'm sold. But, take it slow and easy. Us old-fashioned folk have to be pulled kicking and screaming into the twenty-first century."

Mr. Hanson smiled broadly. "Thank you for being willing to give it a try. Both I and the computer feel much better now."

The lesson continued. Words and symbols flashed across the screen, each representing the awesome power of modern-day computing. Little by little, Martha began to grasp the ins and outs of the new system. About the second week she even admitted, with guarded enthusiasm, that she enjoyed working with "this electronic monster."

The day finally arrived when Mr. Hanson proudly announced to his staff that the New York office of Hanson & Hanson was ready to connect and communicate with Montana—just as soon as he got out there, of course. Martha had conquered the computer age. A happier woman could not be found in all of the city.

The day also finally arrived when the big apartment stood vacant. Everything had been loaded onto the large moving van parked in the alley beside the towering apartment building, ready for transport westward.

Mr. Hanson had rented a small trailer to pull behind his own minivan. In this he placed his precious computer equipment, several items from the apartment that he and the girls had decided would stand a better chance of reaching Montana still in one piece if they took them there themselves, several boxes of clothing, and assorted family treasures collected through years of living in the big city.

Wendy had mailed to Connecticut a detailed map showing her mother the exact location of the ranch, Grandpa and Grandma's phone number and address, and an open invitation to "come anytime, even if it's at 3:00 in the morning."

With a final check around the rooms and the shedding of a few tears, especially on Debbie's part, the trio headed for the lobby and the parking garage.

Slowly they made their way to the Lower East Side, to the dirty street that ran past the abandoned warehouse.

Joey was waiting out on the sidewalk in front of his building, sitting on top of a wooden box.

"What on earth is that?" Mr. Hanson asked, stepping down from the minivan.

"It's my stuff."

The man eyed the box suspiciously. "I had no idea you had so many things to take with you."

"Hey," the boy laughed, "a guy can collect a lot of junk in 15 years."

Mr. Hanson began to drag the heavy box toward the trailer.

"No, wait," Joey called out excitedly, "I want this to ride in the van with me."

"What?" the man gasped. "There'll be no room for you to sit down."

"Oh, sure there'll be. See?" The boy carefully hoisted the box through the open door of the van and jumped in behind it. With a smile he positioned his treasure in the wide space between the seats and threw his legs over it. "No problem," he announced.

The lawyer lifted his hands in frustration. "Well, if you don't mind sitting like that all the way to Montana."

"I don't mind," the boy assured him.

Lizzy walked slowly down the steps and greeted Debbie and Wendy. She hugged Mr. Hanson and then, with a sad smile, lifted her arms toward the boy sitting on the box.

Joey jumped from the van and rushed to his friend. "Now, Dizzy," he said, "the forecast says rain tomorrow, so you'd better get your arthritis pills out. I told Mr. Burnside to stop by every day and check on you. He said he would.

"Mrs. Peterson down the street said she'd call you every afternoon at 3:00 to see if you need anything from the grocery store, and I left you some ice cream in the freezer in my apartment. If you-know-who gives you any trouble, tell her to mind her own business."

Lizzy looked at the boy with tenderness. "You've always taken such good care of this old lady," she said lovingly. "I'll be fine. Thank you, Joey."

The boy pressed close to the woman. "I love you Dizzy," he said softly. "I'll miss you terrible, but I'll write every week. You can count on it."

Lizzy smiled. "I know you will. And Joey," she motioned toward the box in the minivan, "take good care of your treasure."

Mr. Hanson looked at the woman, then at the box stuffed in between the seats. He was about to ask what she meant by her last statement when Lizzy spoke to him.

"You keep an eye on my little Joey," she said. "You're doing a wonderful thing for him." The woman looked warmly at the two girls waiting by the van. "You'll never know how happy you've made me this day. Now, get out of here before I start crying all over the sidewalk."

The little band of travelers hopped into their waiting vehicle. With waves and shouts they moved away from the old woman standing on the sidewalk.

Before long, the towering buildings and mean streets of New York City were just a reflection in the rearview mirror. The escape had begun. The road ran west, toward a land filled with promise, and a life brimming with adventure.

CHAPTER SIX

NOBODY

★ ★ ★

The green, lumpy carpet of grass and trees that forms Pennsylvania spread out from the interstate highway and rolled along beside the minivan as it sped across the summer countryside.

Debbie and Wendy slept soundly, weary from their long days and nights of packing.

But there was no sleep for Joey Dugan. His young face pressed against the cool window glass beside his seat. Every curve in the road, every hill and valley, held for him a breathless mystery of beauty.

Farms that nestled in gentle folds of land seemed so far removed from the city as to represent to him a whole new civilization. Sitting there atop his precious box, the boy marveled at each vision, each wondrous revelation of life beyond the Lower East Side.

Mr. Hanson studied the teenager's form reflected in the rearview mirror. The man smiled. This was what the move was all about. The joy radiating from the young passenger's face filled him with warm feelings. Maybe it was worth the effort. Maybe Montana was a good idea after all.

But there were so many more children like Joey back in the city. He couldn't reach them all. It would be impossible.

Martha's words echoed once again in his thoughts. He could see her kind face looking over at him. "You want to change the world, Tyler?" she'd asked. "Then change a life, just one life. The world will have to adjust."

Renewed determination gripped the lawyer's heart. He and his father would make it work—for Joey, for any child needing to escape.

"Daddy?" Debbie's voice broke his reverie. "Daddy? I think we'd better stop at the next rest area. I need to . . . rest."

Mr. Hanson laughed out loud. "OK. A sign a few miles back said there's one coming up shortly. We'll take a break. All of us can . . . rest."

Wendy stirred. "I'm hungry."

"Imagine that," the man chuckled. "It's still a little early for supper, but I guess you all deserve a treat. You've worked hard getting ready for this trip. I'll see if there's an ice-cream shop where we stop. That'll hold you over until we pull in to a motel for the night."

The two girls looked at Joey. His face was still pressed against the glass.

"Hey, Joey," Wendy called. "You want some ice cream?"

The boy nodded. "Ain't it somethin'?" he asked, wonder filling each word. "So many trees. So much grass. Ain't it just really somethin'?"

Debbie and Wendy giggled. "Yeah, Joey," they said in unison. "It's really somethin', all right."

The boy turned and faced the sisters. "Go ahead and make fun of me. I ain't had too much opportunity of travelin' where it's all green like you two have."

Debbie softened. "We're sorry, Joey. We don't mean to make fun of you. There was a time when we hadn't seen many trees and stuff. Daddy took us for a trip to upstate New York. It kinda took our breath away too."

"Yeah," Wendy added. "I thought cows were big dogs with no hair."

Mr. Hanson burst out laughing. "I remember that. When you finally got close to one, it reached out and licked you on top of the head. You screamed bloody murder. Then you went around telling everyone that the cow was trying to eat you. The farmer said cows ate only grass, but you didn't believe him."

Joey smiled broadly. "Hey, I guess I'm not the only crazy city kid in this car after all."

Wendy thrust her nose into the air. "Well, I'm much older now. I'll bet I could walk right up to a cow and . . . and . . . milk it."

"I'll bet you can," Debbie interjected. "Just make sure it's one with big, long horns. They like to be milked."

Mr. Hanson chuckled. "Now, girls, let's be civil. We all have much to learn about life outside the city. We're not a whole lot different than Joey. We need to support each other, OK?"

"OK," the sisters chorused.

In a few minutes the minivan slipped out of the fast lane of the interstate and drove up the long ramp toward a rest area set amid the trees. Mr. Hanson pulled up beside the gas pumps and shut off the motor. "Now, don't be too long, you guys," he called over his shoulder as he opened his door. "We don't have much . . ."

The back of the van was already empty. "Whew," he breathed. "When you gotta rest, you gotta rest."

Before he'd finished filling the tank with gasoline, the three youngsters had sauntered back to the vehicle.

"Hey, Daddy," Wendy said through the open window. "They've got ice cream inside the store."

"Good," the man announced, placing the gas nozzle back on the pump. "Let me pay my bill then I'll go get us all a little treat."

Debbie, Wendy, and Joey sat discussing the relative merit of every ice-cream flavor known to man until Mr. Hanson appeared at the open door. "OK, travelers," he said enthusiastically, "I'm going to get Fudge Ripple. Now, what do you guys want?"

Voices called out excitedly. "Strawberry!"

"Chocolate!"

"Vanilla!"

"Peach!"

The man turned, repeating the flavors one at a time as he walked toward the store. After a few paces, he stopped. Something was wrong.

Returning to the van he called once more, "What was it you guys wanted?"

Again voices rang out. "Strawberry!"

"Chocolate!"

"Vanilla!"

"Peach!"

The man turned back toward the store, then stopped. "Wait a minute," he said. "How come I get four flavors and there are only three kids?"

Joey squirmed. "I didn't hear four flavors." He kicked the side of the box. "Must be too much noise around. Try it again."

Mr. Hanson paled. "OK," he said slowly. "What do you guys want?"

"Strawberry," Debbie called out, a little unsure of what was going on.

"Chocolate," Wendy added.

"Vanilla," Joey urged.

"Peach."

Mr. Hanson looked at the box resting below Joey. "Did I hear peach?" the man said loudly.

"Yeah, peach," the box responded.

Everyone's mouth dropped open. Joey blinked and gasped. "Hey!" he shouted, "there's somebody in my box. I don't remember packing a person in there!"

"Sure, you don't." Mr. Hanson reached up and pulled the boy from his wooden perch.

He lifted the lid carefully. At first nothing happened. Then, slowly, a little head covered with dark ringlets emerged from inside the colorful pile of socks and shirts. Bright eyes shone above a smile almost as wide as the round face.

Debbie gasped. "There's a little girl in Joey's box!"

Joey fell back against the seat. "Now, how'd that get in there?"

Mr. Hanson reached out and lifted the unexpected passenger from the box and gently set her down on the van's running board.

The girl was dressed in a shirt and jeans. The flowered print of her shirt was faded, but it was clean; the jeans had been patched, obviously by hand. A tiny red bow perched on the top of her head.

She looked first at one astonished face then another. Turning to Mr. Hanson, her smile broadened even further. "I'm 4 years old and I like peach," she said.

The man glared up at Joey. "Well, Mr. Dugan, I

believe you owe me an explanation."

Joey let out a long sigh. "If I had told you about her back in the city, you probably wouldn't have let her come."

"Probably not," Mr. Hanson agreed.

"There, you see?" Joey argued, throwing his hands into the air.

The man studied the little girl's face. "Who is she, Joey? Can you at least tell me that?"

The teenager brightened. "Her name is Samantha. I call her Sam. She's my sister."

"Your sister!" Mr. Hanson said in astonishment. "Joey, she's Black!"

"She is?" the boy recoiled.

"I am?" Samantha gasped.

The man closed his eyes. "Of course she is, I mean, you are." Mr. Hanson ran his fingers through his hair. "Oh, this is ridiculous."

Wendy reached out a hand in Samantha's direction. "Hi, Sam," she said warmly. "I'm Wendy. I didn't know Joey had a sister."

Mr. Hanson glared once again at Joey. "She's not his . . . Mr. Dugan, may I talk with you in private?"

"Sure thing, Mr. H." The boy jumped down from the van. "But can we talk over ice cream?"

"NO!" Mr. Hanson grabbed the boy's arm and began leading him toward the picnic area beside the filling station. "You've got some explaining to do, young man, and you'd better talk fast before I stuff you in that box and ship you back to Lizzy, C.O.D."

"Do I sense a little hostility here?" the boy asked, stumbling along beside the fast-stepping man.

"No, Joey, you don't sense a little hostility. You sense a lot of hostility!" Reaching a picnic table, the

81

man sat Joey down; then he began pacing back and forth.

"I don't believe this," the lawyer muttered. "Joey Dugan, I don't know what to do with you. You're crazy. Totally, unreservedly, undeniably, off your rocker. What in the world made you pack a little Black girl in a box and try to smuggle her to Montana? It's going to take us five days to get there. What was she to do, hibernate in there? Just how did you plan to feed the poor kid, and keep her from suffocating?"

"Hey," Joey shrugged. "There are holes in the box. I put them there, myself. Besides, we'd manage. I've been takin' care of her all her life. Worse things have happened to us."

Mr. Hanson threw up his hands. "No. No! I don't want to hear about it. I've just got to think of a way to get that little girl back to New York before someone accuses me of kidnapping."

"Hey, don't worry," Joey encouraged. "No one knows she's gone. Well, maybe Dizzy."

"Mrs. Pierce knew about this?" The man almost shrieked. "I can't believe it. She *knew*?"

"Yeah. We planned it together. She said you'd understand."

The lawyer stopped pacing. "Oh, she did, did she? Well, you can tell Lizzy Pierce that I don't understand, and you can tell her that just as soon as you get back to New York, because that's where you're going."

The man turned and started toward the van. Joey jumped up and ran after him. "Mr. Hanson, wait. I got to tell you somethin'. You see, there's no one waiting for Samantha back in the city. Her folks are dead. She ain't got nobody. I'm telling you the truth. She ain't got nobody but me."

The lawyer slowed, then stopped. "What do you mean?"

Joey ran up beside him. "Like I said, I'm all she's got in the whole world. Her parents died and I found her in this old apartment when she was just a little baby. She wasn't doing too good so I brought her home to live with me. I fed her milk and Dizzy helped me clean her up and stuff. I've been watchin' out for her ever since."

The boy looked toward the van. "So, I couldn't go off and just leave her alone. She'd cry. I hate to see her cry."

Mr. Hanson studied the teenager's face. He saw desperation in the young eyes, the same kind of look Lizzy Pierce had had that day in the hospital.

"So, you see Mr. H, it's like a package deal. Me and Sam come together, like a team. And I promise, I'll take care of her. She won't be no bother. I'll make sure."

The man felt suddenly tired. "You got any more surprises for me, Joey? You got a 'brother' or something waiting in Montana?"

"No, sir," the lad said solemnly. "No more surprises. Please, Mr. Hanson, I know she's not my sister, not really, but, is it OK if I pretend she is? Sam needs me to be her brother. She ain't got nobody else."

The man hesitated, then spoke slowly. "Joey, sometimes I get the distinct impression I'm not taking you to Montana; you're taking me."

Joey smiled. "Hey, what do I know from Montana?"

Mr. Hanson sighed. "You go back and wait with the girls at the van. I've got to call Captain Abernathy and let him know I found a New Yorker in a box in Pennsylvania. He's going to love this, I'm sure."

Joey started for the minivan, then stopped. "Hey,

Mr. H, you're not so bad for a hotshot lawyer."

The man waved weakly and headed for the store. Joey called after him. "And don't forget the ice cream."

* * * * *

The journey continued westward through Ohio. The land began to relax, preparing itself to become Indiana, with its flat croplands and picturesque farms.

The wide, sweeping plains of Illinois offered up Chicago, bordered on one side by a network of interstates and lesser highways, and on the other by Lake Michigan.

Joey was fascinated by the great number of trucks that sped around the city. He felt sure everyone must have an 18-wheeler as a second car.

Samantha sat on Wendy's lap, surveying the passing scenery. The two girls had formed an immediate and strong friendship since their first meeting in Pennsylvania. Wendy believed it her solemn responsibility to be the mother figure in little Sam's life.

"Do you see that big building over there?" Wendy asked, pointing toward the distant Sears Tower, part of Chicago's famous skyline.

"Yes," Samantha replied.

"Well, that's a very important building."

"Why?" the little girl asked.

"Because," Wendy affirmed.

"Because why?" Samantha pressed.

"Because . . . it's so very big. Big things are always important."

"Oh," Samantha said, "I see. You're very smart, Wendy."

The older girl shrugged. "I do my best."

Wisconsin and Minnesota paraded evergreens, lakes, and the mighty Mississippi past the minivan and its excited passengers.

South Dakota spread like an ancient scroll across the tablelands of Middle America. From their windows, the children saw wheat fields adding their golden touch to the wild, untamed prairie.

The blue waters of the great Missouri River flowed under the speeding vehicle as it swept across the long bridge spanning the waves.

Later that day Mr. Hanson studied the map that lay across his lap; he called out to his passengers, "See that area over there?"

Everyone looked in the direction he indicated.

"Those are the Badlands of South Dakota," he announced.

"What makes them 'badlands,' Daddy?" Debbie wanted to know.

"I guess the pioneers found living there very hard and dangerous. Wild natives, no place to grow food, and harsh weather probably didn't help any, either. So they called it the Badlands."

"Sounds like New York City, if you ask me," Joey said, smiling over at Mr. Hanson. "I thought we were leaving all that stuff behind."

The lawyer chuckled. "We are," he responded, motioning toward the wind-and-weather-sculptured landscape. "See, not a taxicab in sight."

At Rapid City the little caravan turned south for a quick side trip to Mount Rushmore. There the travelers stood gazing up at the faces of four famous American presidents carved into the side of the granite mountain.

Wendy held Samantha up for a better view. "Do you know who those men are?" she asked.

"No," the little girl replied.

"Well," Wendy cleared her throat, "there's Abraham Lincoln, George Washington, Thomas Jefferson, and . . . and . . . some guy with a mustache."

Debbie sidled over to her sister. "That's Theodore Roosevelt, silly. Everyone knows that."

"Well, excuse me, Madam Encyclopedia," Wendy huffed. Turning back to Samantha she said, pointing, "I made a slight error. That's Abraham Lincoln, that's George Washington, that's Theodore Roosevelt, and that's some guy with a mustache."

After a delightful trip through the Black Hills, which Joey insisted should be called the Green Hills because he didn't see anything black about them, the travelers found themselves in Wyoming with its wide, endless plains.

Heading northwest, they crossed into Montana at last. They passed Billings and then Livingston. Mr. Hanson announced, with a sweep of his hand, that beyond the mountains that loomed ahead of them they'd find the city of Bozeman, and just south of Bozeman, journey's end!

Slowly, as they drove along, the land they traveled began to rise. Higher and higher they went; the very air became static with excitement.

To the left of the interstate the children watched strings of diesel locomotives, all hitched together, pulling long trains of swaying box cars along miles of steel track.

"Bozeman Pass," Mr. Hanson encouraged. "We're getting close!"

The road, as if tiring of its climb, began a gentle descent. As the minivan rounded a curve, everyone gasped at once. There, spreading out to distant mountains, was a great and beautiful valley.

"That's it. That's it!" the lawyer called excitedly. "That's Gallatin Valley. Not far from here, we're going to make our new home. Isn't it beautiful? Isn't it just beautiful?"

The children let out a collective sigh. "Oh, Daddy," Debbie said enthusiastically. "It *is* beautiful. And so big! It's like the sky goes on forever."

Mr. Hanson nodded. "Some people call this Big Sky Country. Seems like a good name to me."

Samantha took in the breathtaking vista. "That must be a very, very, *very* important valley," she announced.

The road continued down toward the wide expanse of farmland. Nestled near the base of the mountain range, a town met the wide-eyed gaze of the travelers.

"And that's Bozeman, Montana," Mr. Hanson announced. "We'll come here often to shop and get supplies for the ranch. It's the nearest town to where we'll be living."

Exiting from the interstate, the little minivan and its trailer moved slowly down the main street of town.

The wide avenue was lined with shops, banks, motels, restaurants, and gas stations. Rising head and shoulders above all the other red-and-tan-brick structures was an old building labeled Hotel Baxter.

Every so often, small, evenly-spaced green trees sheltered the sidewalks. They made the town appear warm and friendly, not like rigid, stiff New York City. The traffic flowed along steadily, and no drivers blew their horns in frustration.

"It's so clean," Debbie remarked. "No piles of garbage, no wrecked cars; just neat little streets and neat little stores. I like it. I just wish they had a mall."

As if in answer to her request, a large shopping mall appeared to the right of the road. "Well, OK!" the girl giggled. "I could live here."

Mr. Hanson accelerated as they headed out of town.

"We didn't come to live in another city," he said with a smile. "We're wanting to make our home in the middle of nature."

"Nature's all right," Debbie encouraged, "as long as there's a shopping mall not too far away."

"Spoken like a true city-dweller," the man teased. "You'll change your tune soon enough, . . . I hope."

Out across the flat, wide valley they went. Horses and cows ate contentedly on the green grasses that stretched to the distant mountains.

Turning south on Highway 191, the little minivan drove in the direction of rising terrain. Soon the travelers passed into a world of flowing rivers, towering mountains, and stately trees.

The road wound through high-walled canyons of granite and spruce. It was as if the vehicle had been swallowed by the land and was moving deep into the very bowels of nature.

Mr. Hanson pulled a slip of paper from his pocket and studied the words and lines written there.

"Look for an old barn with a rusted, green Jeep parked beside it," he told the children.

All eyes surveyed the passing scenery. Soon the desired landmark hove into view. Turning left off the main highway, the travelers found themselves on an old, rutted, gravel road that snaked further among the mountains.

Slowly, carefully, Mr. Hanson guided his vehicle along the ancient track, trying to miss the larger of the potholes.

Occasionally the road would skirt a meadow, its green grass and windblown trees shimmering in the sunlight like objects in a living treasure chest.

To the right of the road, a creek slipped in and out of view below overhanging branches and bushes, its waters sparkling silver and white in the clear air.

High above, broad-winged birds could be seen against the deep blue of the sky, their feathered forms held aloft by the currents of air that rose from the deep canyons and tree-lined meadows.

Mr. Hanson suddenly realized no one had spoken for quite some time. He understood. Only the awesome beauty of nature could leave human beings totally without words.

His heart sang silently. The spell had begun. Even now the ranch was reaching out in welcome, calling the weary travelers home.

CHAPTER SEVEN

THE NEW HOME

★ ★ ★

Grandpa Hanson stood on the large front porch of his stately home. His piercing brown eyes, scanning beyond the nearby creek to the distant mountain tops, watched scattered clouds drift in the afternoon sky. Instinctively he drew in a long, deep breath, filling his lungs with the fresh, clean air of his valley.

The elderly man leaned his broad shoulders against the wooden porch railing and looked to his right. He studied the pasture that rose from the edge of a fast-flowing creek. Half a dozen horses grazed beside the fence, their tails twitching occasionally, disturbing the bugs that pestered their broad flanks.

A bridge led from the wide yard, across the creek, to the horse barn and tack building. A saddle straddled the hitching post, its leather smooth and shiny from years of use.

Walking to the other end of the porch, the man looked up toward the road that skirted the side of the hill. That road was his connection to the world beyond his valley. From the main highway it ran along the creek for five miles, slipped by just above his ranch, and continued on to distant mountain passes.

Grandpa Hanson rubbed his chin with a work-worn hand. How many horses and buggies had moved along that road? It used to be part of a stagecoach route from Bozeman to Yellowstone. That's why his home had been built. It had been a way station, a hotel for weary travelers. If only the broad boards and long, hand-formed nails could speak. What stories they could tell—tales of adventure, romance, discovery.

He stepped out into the yard and looked back at his way-station home. Tall chimneys rose from each side of the two-story building, holding the structure upright in their regal embrace. Across the face of the building, broad, rough-wood porches jutted from each floor, giving the dwelling an almost southern air, like a misplaced plantation house.

Oversized windows looked out onto the porches, letting the beauty of the valley with its bright, pure light flood the large sitting room and dining area downstairs and the rows of bedrooms upstairs.

Pushing straight back from both sides of the building were the north and south wings, each holding guest rooms. How sturdy the structure looked; and how homey, too. Montana's winters can be harsh. The old man knew this from experience. He also knew the station had been around longer than he had. If only he could be so strong.

"Willy Hanson, where are you?" A woman called from inside the dwelling. Grandpa smiled. His wife's cheery voice always seemed to fit the warm security he felt each time he walked the grounds of his beloved ranch.

"Dinner's ready," the voice continued, "unless, of course, you don't like mashed potatoes and gravy, in which case I'll give them to the coyotes."

"Don't you dare," the man warned, hurrying in the direction of the porch. "If those critters want something to eat they can have tree bark, not my potatoes."

As Grandpa Hanson reached the steps that led up to the porch his wife appeared at the door.

"Well, come on, old man," she encouraged. "We haven't got all day. Tyler could be here any minute."

The woman moved out into the sunlight. Her silver-grey hair was pulled back from her face and stuffed under a fisherman's hat. She moved with the same sturdy grace Grandpa Hanson had admired the first day he'd met her, back in college. Even now her tanned skin and gentle smile tugged at his heart.

"Just think, Willy," she called to her husband, "our little boy is coming home. Took him long enough to make up his mind. Always has been a hard-headed fellow. Gets that from your side of the family."

"Oh, I just can't wait to see Debbie and Wendy. They've probably grown clean out of childhood, and I had to miss it all."

"I wouldn't worry," the man encouraged as he topped the stairs. "There's plenty of kid left in them. Wendy's only 9 years old!"

"I guess you're right. But they've been so far away." The woman squeezed into her husband's strong arms. "I wanted them out of that city so bad I almost went crazy. Now they're coming here to live on the ranch. It's like a dream come true. Praise the Lord."

The man smiled and hugged his happy wife. "It will be nice to have children around the place. I'm looking forward to that young Dugan fellow helping me out with the ranch. I'm not getting any younger, you know."

Grandma Hanson looked up into the ruddy face and kind eyes of the one who held her. "Oh, you poor baby. Finding it hard to tie your shoes lately?" she teased.

The man laughed. "I can still tie them," he said. "It's just getting harder and harder to make them run after those silly horses out there. Between Tyler and the Dugan boy, I'll just sit on the porch and tell everyone else what to do."

"Sure, you will," the woman teased, taking her husband by the hand and leading him toward the front door. "You'll be out there showing off to anyone who'll watch, just like you've done for 14 years now."

A movement up on the side of the hill caught the couple's eyes. A minivan pulling a trailer edged along in front of a small cloud of dust.

"They're here!" Grandma shouted, racing across the porch and down the steps. "Come on, old man," she called over her shoulder. "They're finally here."

Mr. Hanson and the children looked down from their windows and saw a little valley emerge from behind the trees. At one end of the valley was a beautiful meadow ringed with spruce and multi-hued bushes. A large building, surrounded by a carefully clipped lawn, sat amid aspen groves and flowers. Through the hollow, a creek flowed freely, meandering past a fenced-in field complete with horses, barn, and tack shed. A small footbridge arched across the sparkling waters, connecting the lawn with the horse pasture.

At the far end of the valley, fruit trees grew in ordered rows, their leaves turning gently in the afternoon breezes.

The travelers noticed two figures running from the

large dwelling, their arms waving in the air. Mr. Hanson pressed the minivan's horn, sending a blast of greeting echoing into the mountains.

"There they are! There they are!" the man shouted. "That's Grandma and Grandpa. And that's our new home, kids. Look at it. It's even more beautiful than I remembered."

Cheers rose from the occupants of the vehicle. After the long days of traveling, the journey was ending in a place more grand than any of them had imagined.

At the far end of the hollow the road leveled off onto the valley floor. Mr. Hanson carefully turned off the bumpy track and drove onto the long, narrow driveway. It doubled back and followed the creek past the fruit trees to the broad meadow at the base of the hill.

Grandpa and Grandma were waiting by the grove of aspen trees that guarded one side of the lawn. Debbie and Wendy jumped from the minivan even before it had come to a complete stop. Hugs and kisses were equally distributed among the Hanson family amid shouts of joy and welcome.

Joey and Samantha waited in the vehicle, unsure of what to do. They had never seen family happiness on such a broad scale before. Their faces beamed with joy just watching the jubilant reunion.

Suddenly Grandma looked toward the minivan. "Well, what on earth have we here?" she called out and began walking toward the waiting children, a look of surprise on her face.

"You must be Joey Dugan," she said warmly, extending her hand in greeting. "But who is this beautiful little girl sitting beside you?"

Mr. Hanson and the others joined the woman by the open car door. "Yes, that's Joey, all right," the man said. "And the little tyke is his sister, Samantha."

Grandma blinked. "His sister? But—"

"It's a long story," Mr. Hanson interrupted. "Let's just say our family grew during the trip. I'll tell you all about it later."

"Well, I'm glad to meet you, Samantha," the woman said, smiling. "I'm happy you came to live with us. How old are you?"

Samantha held up four fingers. "I'm 4 years old and I like peach ice cream."

Everyone laughed. "Peach, is it?" Grandma chuckled. "Well, how would you like some homemade ice cream, and on top of it some real peaches from our orchard? None of that store-bought stuff out here. Would you like that?"

The little girl smiled broadly and nodded. "Can I have a big bowl?"

Grandma lifted little Samantha into her arms and held her close. "You can have two big bowls, if that's what you'd like. Why, you're just skin and bones. We've got to fatten you up, you precious child. Come on, everybody, dinner's on the table."

The happy group hurried toward the station, their mouths watering at the thought of home-cooked food after days of restaurant fare.

As they walked along, Wendy kept eyeing the horses that kept abreast of them beyond the fence on the other side of the creek. Grandpa edged over to her. "Looking for something?" he asked.

"Who, me?"

"Yeah. You seem to be checking out the horses very carefully. I thought maybe there was something you were searching for."

Wendy looked up at her grandfather. "Well, I was just trying to see if you had any brown horses, especially one with a white star between his eyes. That's my favorite kind, you know."

Grandpa winked at his son. "Oh, it is? Well, maybe we have one fitting that description around somewhere." The man stopped and the others gathered around, eager to see what would happen next.

"As a matter of fact, there's one particular horse I know of that does everything before all the others. He eats first, sleeps first, wakes up first. I don't know. You probably wouldn't want to see a horse like that, would you?"

Wendy stood on first one foot then the other, excitement almost bursting from her young face. "Yes! That kind of horse sounds just fine to me."

Grandpa pointed toward the group of animals waiting on the other side of the fence. "Do you see him over there?"

Wendy studied the handsome forms with pointed ears and flowing manes. She looked and looked, but there was no brown horse with a white star between his eyes among them.

"Are you sure you have a horse like that?" she urged. "I don't see him over there."

Grandpa rubbed his chin. "Strange. This particular horse always seems to know what's going to happen before it happens. Take that group over there. They're probably thinking that when I get to the footbridge I'm going to stop and feed them some apples from my big pocket. But the brown horse with the white star knows that will happen. So, where do you think he is?"

Wendy stepped away from the cluster of people and looked toward the footbridge. Her face brightened into a flushed smile. *"Early!"* she cried, racing along the creek.

There, waiting patiently on the other side of the

bridge, stood a brown horse with a white star between his eyes.

The girl ran along the yard, jumping over flower beds and sweet smelling bushes. In moments she was racing across the bridge and sliding to a halt in front of the proud animal that waited by the gate.

"Oh, Early," the others heard her say. "You're the most beautiful, wonderful horse in the whole world. I can't believe you're mine, all mine. I just can't believe it!"

The horse tossed his head up and down as if to say, "Well, I'm happy too. I've always wanted a little girl for my very own. We're going to be great friends."

As the family joined the excited girl, Early turned and sped across the pasture, his head held high in joyous abandon.

Wendy climbed up onto the gate and watched her horse prance among the bushes and grass. Her heart overflowed with wonder at the beauty and grace of the animal.

Joey hoisted Samantha up on his shoulders so she could have a clear view of the goings-on. Never before had the two seen such utter freedom, such complete joy.

Early paused in the middle of the pasture and rose on powerful hind legs, his front hooves fanning the air. He seemed to be dancing to some happy melody only he could hear.

Joey looked around at the smiling faces. His eyes passed on to the horse, the pasture, the mountains. New York City seemed a lifetime away.

Years of noise, commotion, and fear began to fade from his thoughts. Was there really a place like the city, or had he been the victim of a bad dream for the past 15 years? This very moment was what mattered most. Here was where he wanted to be. The ranch in the valley was the kind of place he could be proud to call home.

A tiny sadness crowded into the joy he was feeling. In his mind's eye he pictured a little old woman sitting on a rusted chair by a dirty street. He sighed deep within himself. Oh, if only Dizzy could be here to see all this. If only she could smell the nature-scented air and feel the clean sun on her face.

Early pranced back to the gate where Grandpa and the others were waiting. The man reached into the pockets of his overalls and pulled out some apples. He gave one to Wendy, and she held it out toward the horse.

The animal lifted his chin, lips twitching, warm breath whistling from his nostrils. With an easy touch he lifted the fruit from the girl's hand and crunched it in his mouth. He shook his head from side to side as if to say, "Why, that's the best tasting apple I've ever eaten. And I know apples!"

Joey felt a hand on his shoulder. Turning, he looked into the kind face of Grandpa Hanson. "Joey," the man said, "I'm very glad you've joined us here on the ranch. I can tell that you're going to be a good worker. There are many things for you to learn and do here. But most of all, I want you to know you're part of our family now, you and little Samantha. You can stay here as long as you like."

The boy smiled. "I know we'll like it here," he said. "But you'll have to teach me what I'm supposed to do. I don't know nothin' about horses and ranchin' and stuff like that, but I'm willing to learn. And Samantha can work, too. She may be small, but she's very strong."

Grandma joined her husband. "Samantha work?

Nonsense. Her job is to be a little girl. You can work enough for both."

"All right," Joey agreed, "I can do that. And you won't be sorry. I'll do real good." The boy looked out over the pasture. "This is the kind of place I used to dream about—the trees, the flowers, the mountains. I really appreciate you lettin' us come here."

Grandpa nodded. "Then it's settled. As of now, you two are part of the ranch and the Hanson family. As such, you're entitled to three big, delicious, rib-stretching, tummy-bulging meals each and every day."

Grandma gasped. "Dinner! I forgot. Come on, everyone, it's time to eat. I'll set some more places. We have mashed potatoes and gravy, lima beans, fresh spinach, tossed salad, and homemade bread for everyone!"

The group headed for the station, their mouths watering once again with anticipation. The pasture echoed with laughter and shouts. Unpacking and exploring would come later. Now it was time to eat!

* * * * *

The meal was everything the hungry travelers had hoped it would be. Debbie insisted that her figure would completely disappear behind "rolls and rolls of gross, ugly fat" within days.

Wendy especially liked the lima beans. Somehow they tasted better when she knew they'd come from Grandpa's own garden.

Joey held a forkload of spinach up in front of him and studied it carefully. He laughed. "I think I had some of this in a TV dinner once. It didn't have no flavor. This tastes good. Must have been somethin' wrong with my microwave."

Samantha sat proudly between Joey and Wendy. She insisted that her plate be piled as high as everyone else's. "You can't eat all that," Debbie insisted. But she did.

Mr. Hanson recounted the adventures of the journey in great detail. Grandma and Grandpa listened enthralled, especially the part about finding Samantha in Joey's box.

"I called Captain Abernathy last night from the motel," the man reported. "He said he and his men had checked everything out. It's like Joey said. Little Samantha doesn't exist as far as New York City is concerned. He even checked with the local social services agency. They told him it's not uncommon for people to be born, grow up, and die with absolutely no history of them ever being found. It seems incredible, but it's true."

"Well," Grandma said, pouring a glass of milk for herself, "Samantha's history began the day you found her in that box. She's in our family now, as long as she doesn't eat us out of house and home."

The little girl smiled up from her empty plate. "I'm finished," she reported. "Time for dessert."

Everyone burst out laughing and Grandma hurried to the kitchen. She soon returned with bowls of cold, frosty, peach-covered ice cream. It was a perfect finish to a perfect first meal on the ranch.

After the dinner dishes had been cleared and washed, Grandpa took everyone on a tour of the station. He began in the dining room where they had just enjoyed their meal.

"Much of the station's food used to be prepared in the big fireplace," he said, pointing toward the tall, stone-covered hearth. "It also served as a heat source for part of the house.

"The kitchen is big because they fed a lot of people here. I've replaced many of the old washbasins and hand pumps with more up-to-date appliances. Grandma likes the country, but she's pretty spoiled when it comes to modern conveniences."

"You got that right," the woman chuckled. "No scrub boards and outdoor plumbing for me."

Grandpa nodded. "See? I even told her I'd paint the outhouse, but she insisted I work something out here in the station."

The group walked out of the large dining room, through the broad foyer with its two staircases that curved up toward the second floor, and into another spacious chamber. In this room was another huge stone fireplace; the new arrivals also found comfortable recliners, a sofa, and high-back chairs scattered about the room.

A tall wooden bookcase bulged with colorful volumes. Nearby, a checkers board and several game tables stood waiting to entertain during the evening hours.

"This I call the 'sitting room,' although Grandma insists it should be labeled the 'napping room.' Says that's what I use it for mostly."

The woman smiled. "I've even considered naming it the 'snoring room,' but he won't let me."

Returning to the foyer, Grandpa motioned toward the two hallways leading away from the front of the house. "Those go to the bottom floor guest rooms in the north and south wings. The stairways over there take you upstairs to the second floor balcony and the rooms above. It's really simple. You'll learn your way around soon enough.

"Out back, between the two wings, is where I keep my truck and mowing machine. You can park your minivan and trailer there, too, Tyler. Keeps them out of the weather. That's where they used to store stage-coaches and buggies."

The old man looked at his family. "I figure we can all live in the south wing. It's warmer because that section of the station is shielded from the cold winds. During the summer months we'll open up the north wing for our guests. How's that sound?"

Joey and the girls looked puzzled. "Guests? What guests?"

Grandpa Hanson turned to his son in surprise. "You haven't told them yet?"

The man shook his head. "I wanted to wait until we were all together."

Debbie looked suspicious. "When you say guests, do you mean more people are coming here to the ranch?"

Tyler Hanson lifted his hand in the air. "Wait. We'll have plenty of time to discuss this later, after we've unpacked the minivan and trailer." Smiling down at his daughters he added, "I think you're going to like what we have in mind. As a matter of fact, you *have* to like it. We can't pull this thing off without your help."

"Sounds mysterious to me," Wendy mumbled.

"Don't worry, cowgirl," her father urged. "This mystery is kinda neat."

The group made their way out onto the wide veranda and down the steps. The children felt the warm sun on their faces, and the cool breeze that blew from the mountains smelled fresh, invigorating. Whatever the big secret, it must be something nice. After all, they were in Montana.

For the remainder of the afternoon the ranch echoed with the huffing and puffing of hard-working bodies as boxes, suitcases, garment bags, small pieces of furniture, and computer equipment moved from the minivan and trailer to different locations in the station.

Debbie and Wendy were each given upstairs rooms with tall windows that overlooked the creek. Wendy insisted Samantha be allowed to sleep in her room too, so she "could keep an eye on her." The younger sister appreciated the fact that her bedroom window also gave her an unrestricted view of the pasture and horse barn. Every few minutes, she'd drop what she was doing and saunter over to see what Early was up to.

Next to the girls' bed chambers, Mr. Hanson set up housekeeping. His sleeping quarters opened onto a large sitting room at the front of the station. Broad windows and an old wooden door opened out onto the upstairs porch.

He placed his new computer equipment on a strong oak desk near the windows so that he could look up from his work and view the valley, the meandering creek, and the tall, stately mountains in the distance.

Grandpa had already installed a separate phone line for his son to use; he could access his network of legal databases without tying up the station's regular telephone.

Joey found his quarters downstairs by the kitchen. His large room boasted a soft bed, hardwood desk, a closet, wash basin, and his own window overlooking the creek.

One of his main jobs, he was told, was to keep the big fires in the dining and sitting room hearths burning brightly. This wouldn't be much of a chore during the summer months, but when winter captured Montana in its icy grip this particular task would become very important indeed.

Grandpa and Grandma's portion of the station took up the remainder of the south wing's downstairs area.

The old man had built an ample supply of bathrooms on both floors, so everyone would be comfortable.

The bulk of the Hanson family things would arrive from New York in a few days. By telephone the lawyer reserved storage space in Bozeman where his possessions could be stored after the moving van brought them into town. A large 18-wheeler would find it impossible to get from the highway to the ranch.

Mr. Hanson would ride into town with Grandpa on his weekly trip for supplies, and bring back a dresser, a table, or whatever they had room for. He figured the job would be finished in a month or two. The man told his daughters to think of it as an extended Christmas—something more arriving every week.

It was a weary group that finally flopped down onto porch chairs at the end of the day. Activity in the kitchen sent inviting aromas through the station and out onto the broad veranda.

"I'm too pooped to eat supper," Debbie sighed. "But whatever she's baking, it sure smells good."

Wendy moaned. "I think my arms and legs are about to fall off. I'm short enough as it is. All this work won't help."

Joey stretched and yawned. "You girls are just too sissy for all this ranch stuff. I could work five more hours and not even break a sweat."

The two sisters looked at the boy, then at each other. "What do you think, Wendy," the older asked, "should we beat him up now or later?"

"Later," came the weak reply. "Much later."

Samantha walked out onto the porch. "Hey, everybody," she called, "do you like bread with jam on it?"

Joey studied the small form standing in the doorway. "That wouldn't be peach jam, would it?" he queried.

"How did you know?" The girl's smile faded. "It was a secret. Did Grandma tell you?"

"No, half pint; you have peach jam smeared all over your face."

The girl ran a sleeve across her mouth. "Oh, well," she said, "now you know the surprise. But you don't know about the chocolate cake!" She paused. "Oops."

The older children laughed. "Some secret-keeper you are," Wendy said. "That's OK, Samantha. I didn't hear you mention the you-know-what cake."

"Good," the little girl beamed. "See, I can keep a secret." With that she turned and headed back into the station.

Mr. Hanson walked around the side of the building and sat down on the bottom step. "Well, the minivan and trailer are empty and parked behind the house. My computer equipment is installed and ready to roll. Now, if I can just muster up enough energy, I'll rise and . . . walk up those stairs. Yup. That's exactly what I'll do."

Joey moved to the railing and looked out over the peaceful valley. Like Grandpa earlier in the day, he drew in a deep breath and let it out slowly. "This place kinda gets to you," he said. "First you see how beautiful everything is, then you start to feel a strange feeling. I don't know how to explain it. The sky, the mountains, they just reach out and make you happy. Weird."

"Not too weird," Grandpa's voice called from the doorway. "What's strange is that more people don't move to this state. There's lots of room."

"Yeah," Joey countered as he sat down on the bench by the railing. "But they don't have an opportunity like us. I mean, there's tons of guys in my neighborhood who'd give their last dime to come out here."

"Oh?" the old man said smiling. "So, you think if we invited them to come, they would?"

"Are you kidding?" the boy gasped. "They'd steal the first car they could find."

"I believe that!" Mr. Hanson said, rising to his feet. "And they'd all bring big wooden boxes filled with their buddies."

Joey chuckled. "Now, Mr. H, are you ever going to forgive me for bringing little Sam along?"

The man nodded slowly. "I probably would've done something similar if I'd been in your shoes. Besides, Samantha can be useful here. She can build fences, plow the fields, do a little logging."

Grandpa laughed. "Don't listen to him, Joey," he urged. "He did do the very same thing you did. He just didn't stuff you in a box."

"Hey, yeah," the boy agreed. "And I really appreciate that, Mr. H. I'd get claustrophobic." Joey turned to the two girls sitting by the stairs. "I bet you didn't think I knew that word, claustrophobic."

Debbie smiled. "You're a veritable fountain of verbal metaphors."

"And don't you forget it," the boy responded slowly and a little quizzically.

Wendy lifted her hand for silence. "Wait a minute. I think I just figured something out." She looked first at Grandpa, then at her dad. "I get it. You want to invite city kids to come out here to the ranch. That's why we're here, right?"

Debbie's eyebrows rose. "Yeah. You've got the whole north wing of the station standing there totally empty. We fix it up, put in some beds, get a couple more horses, and, bingo, instant dude ranch for kids."

Joey jumped to his feet. "Is that really what's going on? Really?"

Mr. Hanson smiled. "The secret's out. Yes, that's exactly what we have in mind for the summer months."

The children's eyes opened wide. "You mean we're going to have kids come out here every year?" they cried with growing excitement. "This is cool. This is totally cool. When do we start?"

"Next summer," Mr. Hanson said. "If we can have everything ready in time."

"We can do it," Debbie assured him. "We know we can!"

"It's not going to be all fun and games," Grandpa warned. "Running a ranch for city kids takes hard work and real, honest dedication to make it happen."

"Don't worry about a thing," Wendy stated. "We're up to it. You'll see."

"But there's just one problem," the old man said thoughtfully. "We don't have a name for our ranch. We can't ask kids to leave house and home and come out to just 'the ranch.' Sounds boring, don't you think?"

Debbie, Wendy, and Joey thought for a long moment. "Yeah," the boy agreed. "We need a name for this spread. What do you call it, Grandpa Hanson?"

"I just call it 'the ranch.'"

Everyone sat thinking. The evening sun slipped silently behind the mountains back of the house, sending golden shafts of light arching across the darkening sky.

Grandma appeared in the doorway, holding a mixing bowl in her hands. "What's going on?" she asked.

No one spoke.

"I know," she said moving toward the railing. "You're enjoying the evening air. Isn't it lovely out in the valley? Just look at those mountains, how the sun barely touches them with light. And the creek. I love how it moves in and out of the evening shadows. Very romantic, don't you agree?"

Debbie looked up at her grandmother, then out across the meadow. The creek twisted and turned, its laughing waters appearing and disappearing in the lengthening shadows cast by the tall trees and distant mountains.

"What did you just say, Grandma?" the girl asked, rising to her feet.

"I said I like the way the creek moves in and out of the shadows. See? Isn't it lovely?"

Wendy rose slowly. "Yes. Yes," she repeated.

Joey's mouth dropped open. "That's it!" he cried.

"What's it?" Grandma asked.

"That's the new name for our ranch," Debbie said breathlessly.

Grandpa walked to the railing and studied the meadow. "Yes, it's perfect. It's just perfect."

"What's perfect?" Grandma urged. "Will someone please tell me what's going on around here?"

Mr. Hanson ran up the steps and encircled his mother in his arms. "Don't you see? That's the name of our new home. Now we can invite kids to come here with style."

The man ran back down the steps and out onto the wide yard. "Children of the cities," he called, his voice echoing across the valley and high into the mountains. "Welcome, one and all. Welcome, to *Shadow Creek Ranch!*"

CHAPTER EIGHT

"Dear Mom"

★ ★ ★

Wendy awoke slowly. She wasn't sure, but it seemed like there had been a noise outside, like an early-morning bird call, or perhaps a squirrel chirping somewhere deep in the forest behind the station. All she knew for sure was she was waking up.

The girl yawned deeply and opened her eyes. The room was still dark. She turned her face toward the window, where she could see a faint glow to the east—a hint of approaching dawn.

No one in the big house was awake yet. Little Samantha lay sleeping in her bed by the far wall. The only sound Wendy could hear was the slow ticking of the big clock down in the foyer, at the bottom of the curving staircase.

The young girl loved the early morning hours— that time between sleep and dawn when everything was still and she could lie thinking her own thoughts, dreaming without interruption about life as she wished it could be.

Wendy eased out of bed and stood gazing through the window. A movement in the pasture caught her eye. Yes, there was Early, up before everyone else, sampling the dew-covered grass in the deep moonlit shadows at the base of the hill.

The girl smiled. She and her precious horse had a lot in common. They both needed time to themselves. For Wendy that time was early in the morning, while the rest of the world slumbered.

On the small wooden desk at the foot of the bed a portable cassette tape recorder sat amid scattered papers and colorful drawings of trees and horses. The machine contained a partially completed tape.

Wendy studied the tiny microphone that rested beside the recorder. She wondered how many other 9-year-olds had to rely on such an invention to fulfill their need to talk to someone they loved. It didn't seem right. But it was all she had for the moment.

The girl sat down quietly and picked up the little recorder. After rewinding the tape she turned the volume control knob to its lowest setting so as not to disturb the sleeping Samantha. Then she gently pressed "Play." Her own young voice sounded from the tiny speaker, recounting the words she'd recorded the previous night, before sleep had taken her away.

"Dear Mom," she heard herself say. "I know I haven't talked to you for a little while, ever since that first tape I recorded right after we got here. But you wouldn't believe how busy we are.

"For the past two weeks we've had lots and lots of stuff to do here on Shadow Creek Ranch.

"Dad and Grandpa have gone into Bozeman several times to get our furniture and other things for the ranch. You know that dresser you bought for me when I was 6 years old? Well, it's sitting right here in my room next to the door. I've got your picture in a gold frame up on top of it. That way, I see you every time I come in or go out of the room.

"Samantha says you look like a movie star. I told her that you were even more beautiful in person.

"As I mentioned in my first tape, Debbie's room is right next door to mine. She put up yellow curtains at her windows and they look pretty.

"Oh, I must tell you about Early. I hope you don't get tired of me bragging about him, but he's such a wonderful horse.

"Grandpa let me ride him for the first time. We didn't run or anything like that. Early just walked around the pasture with me on him. I felt like I was w-a-y up in the air. It was very exciting.

"Tomorrow, Grandpa says maybe we can get up to a trot. I think Early is tired of just walking around. I know I am.

"Little Samantha likes to sit on the fence and watch me ride my horse. She waves her arms in the air and says, 'Giddy up, giddy up.'

"I asked her if she wanted to take a turn on Early. She said, 'No way. I just want to ride the fence. It doesn't bounce so much.'

"I laughed and laughed at Joey the other day. The first time Grandpa told him to go out and feed the horses, Joey went to the kitchen and got an armful of bread. Grandma wanted to know what he was doing with all her baking. He said he was going out to feed the horses, like Grandpa had told him to. He didn't know horses ate only certain kinds of food. He knows now!"

Wendy heard her voice pause, then continue.

"Do you ever think of me? I mean, like, when you're not busy and running around shopping and stuff? Do you ever think about when you lived with me and Debbie and Daddy in New York? I think about it a lot.

"Grandma is teaching me how to cook. She's teaching Debbie, too. Well, Debbie knows how to make a bunch of different kinds of foods, but Grandma is showing us how to make stuff from the garden. You know, stuff that doesn't come in a can? I think food that comes right from the garden tastes very good.

"Three nights ago we had artichokes. You boil the whole thing and put it in a dish. Then you dip the little leaves in a sauce and scrape off the artichoke food with your teeth. Joey said he'd never eaten a bush before.

"All of us kids have chores to do everyday. Debbie helps Grandma in the kitchen and mows the lawn. Joey takes care of the horses, makes sure the fences and gates are all strong, goes around with Grandpa cutting down dead trees that they make into firewood, and lifts heavy things around the house. He works very hard and says he's getting muscles all over his body.

"Samantha usually tags along with me. That's OK, because I like taking care of her. She's funny.

"My chores are helping to wash the dishes. We have a bunch of dishes around here. Grandma has some pretty plates and I've only dropped one since I started helping. That's pretty good for me.

"I separate the trash. Some gets burned out behind the station, some goes in one bag, and some goes in another. Grandpa says we're helping the world stay clean. When you live in Montana, you want the world to stay clean because it's really beautiful when it is.

"I also help Grandma in the garden. Last Thursday

112

we picked a great big bucket of corn. Then we had some for supper.

"Daddy has his computer equipment all set up and works hard in his new office. I hear him in there sometimes when I walk by. We know that when he's working we're not supposed to bother him.

"Once Samantha went into his office and fell asleep in the chair by the window. Daddy didn't even know she was there."

The voice on the tape ended. Wendy stopped the recorder and stared at it for a long moment. She felt sad, the same sadness she experienced every time she talked to her mother in far away Connecticut.

Rising, the girl walked to the dresser and took down the picture in the gold frame. A blonde, blue-eyed woman sat on a sofa, smiling back at her.

Wendy reached out and ran her fingers along the glassy cheek of the image. She looked into the eyes of the picture, searching, as she always did, for that tiny spark of love she remembered seeing in her mother's face.

But the picture never changed. The eyes in the image were always laughing just the same, every time she looked at it. Was it something she'd just said that made the woman laugh? Had someone told a funny story? She couldn't remember.

The young girl sighed. All she had left of her mother was a picture of her laughing, and she didn't even know why.

Returning to the desk, Wendy picked up the tiny microphone and pressed the "Record" button on her machine. She spoke softly in the gentle light of dawn.

"Mom, I just want you to know that I love you. Sometimes I miss you so much it makes me cry a little. But Daddy says I should be happy that you are happy.

113

Even though I ask him many times, he never can tell me how I'm supposed to do that.

"Please write to me here in Montana. I read your last letter a million times. I love you.

"Early says hello.

"Your little girl, Wendy."

CHAPTER NINE

TAR BOY AND WRANGLER BARRY

★ ★ ★

Joey stood by the barn door, thoughtfully studying the animals. His work was done for the day, the supper bell hadn't rung yet, and everybody else was in the station. The pasture was empty except for the horses and himself.

"I gotta do this," he mumbled. "Debbie and Wendy probably think I'm chicken, so I gotta do this."

Words Grandpa Hanson had spoken earlier that day rang in his ears: "If something makes you afraid, it's best to confront it head on. Look it straight in the eye. Let it know who's boss. That's the only way to conquer fear."

The boy nodded and walked into the barn. He took a bridle down from its hook, lifted a saddle and blanket from a sawhorse by the window, and moved back out into the barnyard.

A group of horses grazed by the cottonwoods. Joey set his feet apart, thrust out his chest, and called, "Hey, you guys, come here!"

The animals' heads swung up. They glanced at the boy holding a saddle. Then they lowered their heads again and continued grazing.

Joey took in a deep breath. "I said, come *here!*" he called firmly.

Again the animals looked over at him. They sniffed the air, thinking perhaps the boy was waiting to give them a little treat. Several even moved a few steps toward him, then they shook their heads as if to say "I don't smell any apples. Do you smell any apples?"

Once more the horses turned, lowered their graceful necks, and continued munching on the grass at their feet.

Joey wondered what to do next. How did Grandpa Hanson get those dumb animals to come to him?

Wait. The old man whistled. Yeah, that's it. He whistled one long, loud note. They always came running when he did that.

Puckering his lips and taking in another deep breath, the lad let loose a piercing trill that sounded more like a teakettle coming to boil than a horse call.

Heads came up quickly this time, and ears pointed forward. In an instant the animals raced toward the astonished boy, more out of curiosity than anything else. They wondered what on earth could make such an awful noise.

Joey took a few steps backward as the thundering hooves drew nearer. Suddenly he was surrounded by heavy-breathing steeds, all looking at him as if to say "Did you just whistle or are you about to boil over?"

The boy cleared his throat. "Good horses," he said, trying to calm his racing heart. "Thanks for coming. I appreciate that very much."

A large black horse Joey had heard Grandpa Hanson call "Tar Boy" stepped from the circle and moved close to him. The animal stretched out his long neck and blew hot breath across the boy's forehead.

Joey reached up slowly and slipped the bridle over the animal's nose, making sure the bit went into the horse's mouth straight, like he'd seen Wendy do time and time again with Early.

At that moment Tar Boy's ears reversed direction and he stood stock still. Even his tail stopped twitching.

Joey, encouraged by this sudden sign of what he supposed to be acceptance, lifted the blanket and saddle and tossed it across the big animal's back.

"Now, Tar Boy," he said, mimicking the soft tones Wendy used, "let me just get this stuff straightened around here and we'll go for a little ride."

Joey made all the connections, just as Grandpa and Wendy had done many times before. He knew this strap went here, that piece of leather slid around there, and this buckle connected to that buckle.

While all this was going on, the horse remained frozen in place. Only its big, dark eyes moved, watching the boy carefully.

With confidence building each second, Joey finally had everything where he thought it should be. Lifting his foot high into the air, he slipped it into the left stirrup. Grabbing the saddle horn, he hoisted himself up and sat straddling Tar Boy's broad back.

"So far, so good," Joey said quietly. "Now, let's see. I hold this long strap in my left hand, and this other strap in my other hand. All right! Hey, I'm doing pretty good."

Leaning forward in the saddle, the boy said softly, "OK, Tar Boy. Mush."

Nothing.

Joey leaned farther forward. "Hey, horse. I'm ready. You can go now."

Still nothing.

Then he remembered something he'd seen Grandpa do on another of the ranch's horses. He lifted the long strap that dangled from his hand high into the air. With a resounding *slap* he brought the leather down onto Tar Boy's flank.

To Joey it seemed like the ground simply dropped away from below the horse. Then it came back *fast*.

With a horrendous jolt, Tar Boy arched his back and flew sideways across the barnyard. Joey's hands gripped the saddle horn in a deathlike embrace, his knuckles turning white, and his face, too.

Next, the horse seemed to explode in all directions at once. The boy saw hooves, legs, tail hairs, and a dark mane flapping in random sequences to the left, right, up, down, and sideways. He realized he no longer had any say in what was about to happen. He'd become a passenger on the wildest ride west of the Mississippi.

Joey opened his mouth to shout but a bone-bending jolt shut it tightly. With a powerful thrust the animal lifted itself and its passenger high into the air. He sailed across the gate that guarded the pasture and stumbled over the footbridge. Seeing open country, he lowered his head and started running.

Faster and faster the horse sped. Joey saw the station whiz by off to one side. Throwing away any vestige of pride he had left, he cried out in a voice very much like a scream: "HELP ME! SOMEBODY H-E-L-P!"

Debbie, who was just passing by the front door on

her way to the sitting room, heard the frantic call. Glancing out the door, she saw a large horse carrying a boy away from the pasture and toward the orchard at the far end of the meadow.

"Hey!" the girl screamed. "Everybody, come quickly. There's a big horse stealing Joey!"

Grandpa ran in from the kitchen. "What'd you say?" he asked.

Debbie pointed in the direction of the fleeing animal. One look told the old man the complete story.

"Oh, my, my!" he shouted. "Tyler! Come quickly. Joey's in trouble. We've got to catch him. Hurry!"

Grandpa Hanson raced down the porch steps, his son not far behind. The two men dashed over to the old farm truck, which was resting in the shade of an aspen tree. They jumped in and started the motor. In a cloud of dust the battered vehicle spun around over the loose gravel and down the driveway in the direction of the charging horse and its rider.

Joey leaned as far forward on the animal as possible. He could feel the powerful cadence of the hoofbeats and the tremendous thrust generated by the hind legs of the horse. He'd never been so frightened in all his life—not even the time when that gang from East Village had come down his street looking for him. They thought he'd told the police about their little "party" at the Post Avenue Deli the night before. Truth was, Joey had been nowhere around. Someone had started the rumor, trying to get him in trouble. Right at this moment, that East Village gang looked like a gaggle of choir boys compared to Tar Boy.

The road led away from Shadow Creek Ranch and along the floor of the valley to the point where the valley narrowed. Then it began to rise gently toward a mountain range that towered in the distance.

Through the trees whipping by, the boy could see jagged rocks and white-foamed streams. Joey closed his eyes. Yup. New York was looking better all the time.

Grandpa and Mr. Hanson jolted across the uneven track, the farm truck skidding and slipping around corners, over potholes and roots. Every once in a while they could see the horse and its rider up ahead. Neither man spoke. They each knew the danger Joey was in. Unconsciously they leaned forward in their seats, as though urging the truck to go faster, faster.

Joey saw the road turn and start a steeper climb up the side of the hill. Tar Boy ignored the bend and swept out into a little clearing. Tall rocks and trees stood at the far end. At their base a small pond rested in the afternoon shadows, its waters glassy smooth.

The farm truck followed close behind, its motor straining. Grandpa Hanson shouted over to his son, "This is a closed canyon. There's no way out. I think we've got him now!"

Where the rocks and trees blocked the headlong path of the big horse the animal slid to a halt. Joey felt himself slipping from the saddle. At that instant the horse reared up on its strong hind legs and let out a long, loud whinny.

The next thing the boy knew he was alone in the air. There was no longer any horse between his legs.

He saw a small pond rising up to meet him, then, *splash!*

The farm truck skidded sideways as it came to rest beside the pond. Even before the vehicle had stopped Mr. Hanson was out the door, running through the water toward the spot where Joey had disappeared.

The teenager felt something grab him around the waist. Thinking it was the big black horse, he fought with all his might. Water flew this way and that as the boy struggled. Then he heard someone calling his name.

"Joey. Hey, Joey. It's me. It's me!"

The boy coughed hard, trying to get air past the water in his throat.

"It's OK, Joey," the man urged. "You're all right now. Just relax. You're safe."

The boy stopped struggling and looked up into the frightened face of Mr. Hanson. "The horse," he sputtered. "Where's the horse?"

"Grandpa's got him," the man said. "He can't hurt you now. It's over. Are you OK?"

Joey stood drunkenly to his feet, water draining from his shirt. Together he and Mr. Hanson waded out of the pond and stumbled over to where the older man waited by the truck. Tar Boy had been tied to a nearby tree.

"Joey," the old man called, his voice shaking with concern. "Are you all right?"

The boy nodded. "I'm OK, Grandpa Hanson. Just kinda wobbly. I think I need to sit down for a minute."

The three dropped onto the running board of the farm truck and sat in silence for a long moment. Grandpa Hanson shuffled his feet in the grass. "Joey, I'm so sorry about what happened. It's a miracle you weren't badly hurt. I don't think I've ever prayed so much in all my life."

The teenager looked up in surprise. "You prayed? For me?"

"Of course," the old man said, still shaken. "I always pray when I feel helpless. There was nothing I could do to help you, so I asked God to step in. I think He did."

The boy blinked. "I never had nobody pray for me before."

Mr. Hanson cleared his throat. "I'm afraid you have."

"You too, Mr. H? You prayed for me?"

"Yeah, back in New York, when you were hurt. I felt kinda helpless too, just like my dad just now." The man smiled. "I hope you don't mind."

Joey laughed. "Hey, I don't mind. I mean, if you think God cares what happens to bad-boy Joey Dugan, then be my guest. Makes me feel good inside that you would do that for me. Yeah. I like what you did." He looked at Mr. Hanson, then at the old man. "Thanks."

The boy leaned his head back against the truck door. "But there's one thing I don't understand."

"What, Joey?" Grandpa Hanson asked.

"Well, that silly horse," the boy continued. "I did everything right, just like I've seen you and Wendy do. I thought me and him were gettin' along fine. Then, *pow,* off he goes like a crazy, mixed-up rocket ship. I mean, I didn't say, 'Hey, horse, jump straight up in the air, turn around a few times, go sailing over the fence, and scare the life out of me.' I didn't say that, but that's exactly what happened."

Grandpa smiled. "You did do everything right. See, the saddle is still on him, the bridle looks good. But you overlooked one small detail."

"What?" Joey asked, his eyes filled with question.

Grandpa Hanson cleared his throat. "You see, Joey, Tar Boy has never been ridden before."

Mr. Hanson gasped. "You're kidding," he said. "Never?"

Joey looked over at the old man. "That's bad?"

Grandpa Hanson chuckled. "Yeah, that's bad, unless you're a very experienced rider who knows how to break horses."

"I sure didn't know how to brake Tar Boy," the teenager said solemnly. "Why, I couldn't get that animal to stop for love or money."

The two men burst out laughing. "Joey," the older man said, trying hard to be serious. "I don't mean brake as in 'come to a stop,' I mean break as in 'to train.'"

Grandpa Hanson and his son held their stomachs as they rocked back and forth, sending gales of mirth into the air. Even Tar Boy shook his head up and down as if joining in the glee.

Joey sat dripping wet. He wasn't quite sure what was so funny. But the two men and Tar Boy looked like they were having such a good time, he decided the joke must be hilarious, so he started laughing too.

Their joyous merriment drifted through the little clearing, across the pond, and into the deep forest where furry creatures and feathered choristers added their voices to the happy sounds.

* * * * *

Wendy's mouth dropped open in utter shock. "You rode which horse?"

Joey flopped down across the sitting room sofa and let out a long sigh. "Tar Boy. You know, that big black beast out in the pasture."

The girl blinked twice. "And you're still alive?"

"I think so," the teenager laughed. "At least parts of me are. Other sections of my body feel kinda dead. I can't get my knees to come together anymore. I think my legs are permanently bent."

Debbie entered the room carrying a large glass of orange juice. "Well, look who's returned from the trail—The Lone Dugan. Did you have a good ride?"

The boy smiled weakly. "Sure. Piece of cake. Tar Boy and I got along fine. We're going to go riding tomorrow at the same time. He likes me."

"Oh, no, you don't," Grandpa Hanson called out as he walked into the room. "Although I must say you handled that horse pretty good for a first-time rider. You're a natural. I'm proud of you, Joey Dugan."

The teenager beamed. "Do you really think so?"

"Yeah, I really think so," the old man encouraged. "I can't say much about your choice of horse, though. Let's not try that again until Barry's had a chance to work his magic on Tar Boy for a couple days."

"Barry?" Debbie queried. "Who's he?"

Grandpa Hanson sat down in his favorite chair by the window. "Barry Gordon is one of Montana's best wranglers. He knows horses like your father knows courtrooms. There's never been a horse young Barry couldn't break . . ." Glancing at Joey the man continued, "I mean, train. He's simply the best there is."

Debbie took a sip from her glass. "How old is this young Barry?"

Grandpa scratched his chin. "Oh, I'd say he's 19, 20."

The girl's eyes opened wide. "Really?" Pausing, she quickly regained her composure. "I mean, he must be very competent."

Grandpa smiled. "He's good-looking, too. All the girls think so. They say he's, how do they put it, super cool."

Debbie lifted her chin a little. "And I'll bet he knows it, too. I hate guys who think they're cool."

"That's what the girls say, not Barry," the old man assured his granddaughter. "He's very humble. A nice guy."

"I'll bet," Debbie snorted as she rose to leave. "I'm not impressed."

"But you haven't even met him yet," Grandpa argued. The young girl ignored the comment and left the room.

Turning to Joey, the old man sighed. "I'll never understand the female mind."

"I'd rather try to ride Tar Boy than do that," the teenager chuckled.

Wendy stood and headed for the door, too. "Well, I think Debbie's right," she retorted. "Barry must be some kind of stuck-up bozo, if you ask me."

Grandpa Hanson and Joey watched her strut from the room. They looked at each other and lifted their hands in frustration. Barry Gordon already had two enemies on Shadow Creek Ranch and he hadn't even shown his face yet.

The very next morning, a four-wheel-drive truck rumbled down the long driveway and stopped near the front of the house. The door of the vehicle opened and out stepped a tall, slim, handsome young man with sun-streaked brown hair and blue eyes. He glanced out across the creek into the pasture. A small herd of horses grazed in the shade of the cottonwoods.

With steady pace the newcomer crossed the lawn and climbed the steps leading to the station's wide porch. At the entrance to the building he paused and knocked firmly.

A little girl pushed the door open and stood looking up at the stranger.

"Who are you?" Samantha asked.

The young man, taken back by the sight of a petite child wearing a cowboy hat almost as wide as she was tall, laughed out loud. "Oh, my," he chuckled, "I think there's a big hat about to eat you up."

Samantha studied the stranger towering above her. "I like this hat," she said. "It doesn't eat people."

"Good," the visitor replied, studying the little girl. "So, are you in charge here?"

Samantha grinned. "I make cookies and ice cream. Do you like peach?"

"Love it." The young man looked past his greeter and glanced around the foyer. "Is Mr. Hanson here?"

"We got two. Which one you want?"

The visitor blinked. "Oh, well, either one will do."

"Wait here," the little girl said, closing the door.

The stranger smiled and walked to the wooden railing. He looked out over the valley toward the distant mountains. A hawk soared in the morning air far above the pines, searching for breakfast among the rocks and grass below.

"May I help you?" a voice cut through the stillness of the ranch. Turning, the young man saw an older gentleman in the doorway.

"Are you Mr. Hanson?" he asked.

"You're probably looking for my father," the lawyer said cheerfully. "Come, I'll take you to him. He's out in the barn."

The two walked down the porch steps and headed for the footbridge.

"I didn't catch your name," the older man said, extending his hand. "I'm Tyler Hanson. My father owns this spread."

"Glad to meet you, Mr. Hanson," the visitor said politely. "I'm Barry Gordon."

"Oh, Barry. Yes. My father called you last night. Thanks for coming out on such short notice."

"No problem," the young man assured his companion. "Your dad sounded a little concerned on the phone. Said you folk needed a horse broken right away."

Mr. Hanson smiled. "Well, it's more of a precaution than an emergency. We have several youngsters here on the ranch who are new to country life. We want to make sure all our horses know how to behave."

The lawyer studied the visitor carefully. "You do this sort of thing for a living?"

"Well, kinda," Barry said. "I'm a student at Bozeman State University, studying agriculture. I break horses as a means of earning a little money on the side. People seem to be happy with my work. I live on a ranch north of town. Been around horses all my life."

The two reached the entrance of the barn and entered through the open door. Grandpa Hanson and the girls were over by one of the stalls, repairing a torn saddle stirrup.

"Dad?" Mr. Hanson called. "Barry Gordon's here."

"Wonderful," the old man said, laying down his tools and walking toward the two standing in the doorway.

"Hi, Barry," Grandpa Hanson said, extending his hand. "We met about a year ago at the fair. I watched you work. Quite impressive."

"Hello again." Barry shook the old man's hand. "Thanks for noticing."

"These are my two granddaughters, Debbie and Wendy." Grandpa pointed toward the stalls. "Come on out here and meet Barry," he called to the girls.

Debbie turned and started walking toward the group by the door. She could see a tall, slender stranger standing between her father and Grandpa. They were all silhouetted against the bright Montana sun.

As she approached, the stranger stepped forward, entering the shadows where she could see him better.

"Hello," he said, his voice cheerful and rich.

127

The girl stopped in her tracks. This was no stuck-up wimp. The face was open, kind, and very, very handsome.

"Heh . . . Heh . . . Hello," she said, wishing she could close her mouth. "I'm meet to glad you . . . I mean . . . I'm glad to meet you."

Barry smiled a broad, unconstrained smile. His white teeth were straight, his eyes sparkled. Debbie felt suddenly weak in the knees.

"You have saddle wax on your face," the new arrival said. "You'd better get it off. It might stain."

The girl blushed. "Oh. Yes. I'll go do that right now. Will you excuse me?"

"Sure," the young man said. "Use lots of soap."

Debbie raced out the door and hurried toward the pump by the tack house, where a large bar of soap waited for just such occasions.

Barry watched her go, his eyes following her thoughtfully.

"Hello." Another female voice interrupted his thoughts. "I'm Wendy and I don't have saddle wax on my face, thank you very much."

The young girl marched past the visitor and strode out of the barn in the direction of her sister.

"Pleasure to meet you," Barry called after her.

The girl ignored him.

"What'd I say?" the young man asked, rejoining the men at the door.

Mr. Hanson and Grandpa chuckled. "It's a long story. Come on, Barry," the old man said. "We've got work to do. We can all try to figure women out later."

"Don't hold your breath," the younger Mr. Hanson laughed.

The three made their way into the pasture toward the circle of horses. "I only have six horses right now," the older man was saying. "In the spring, I'm going to purchase about a dozen more. They will all need to be broken so children can ride them safely.

"Now, that brown horse with a star—his name is Early—he's no problem. Those two over there and the bay have been trained also.

"My biggest concern right now is the black one. We call him Tar Boy. He took our new ranch hand for a real ride last evening. Wasn't the horse's fault, really. Young Joey Dugan didn't know that he'd never been ridden before."

Barry whistled softly. "He's quite an animal, all right. He'll make a fine riding horse. Look at those powerful shoulder and leg muscles. He's proportioned good, too. A real beauty."

Grandpa Hanson smiled. "I can see you know your business. Come, let's head back to the barn and talk money. If we can work out something we both can benefit from, we'll have lots of work for you in the coming seasons."

"Sounds good to me," Barry encouraged. "You do have a beautiful spread here." Catching sight of Debbie walking toward the station, he added. "And real nice scenery too."

Grandpa and Mr. Hanson smiled. "We have only the best here on Shadow Creek Ranch," the old man agreed.

CHAPTER TEN

PARTNERS

★ ★ ★

Joey sat on the fence, watching Tar Boy trot around and around in a circle. The horse's harness was connected to a long rope, the other end of which was held tightly by the wrangler. The young man stood in the middle of the circle, calling out to Tar Boy in soft, encouraging tones.

"Good horse," the young man repeated as he carefully watched the animal trot at the other end of his tether. "You're doing just fine, Tar Boy. You're a beautiful animal, all right. I like the way you move."

Tar Boy shook his head from side to side and snorted, his heavy hooves vibrating the ground with each step. Joey could feel the fence shake gently as the big horse swept past his lofty perch.

"Why you doing that?" he called out to Barry. "You trying to make him dizzy?"

The wrangler laughed. "No, Joey. I'm getting him

used to his harness, and used to being tied to this rope."

Tar Boy snorted again. The man in the circle watched carefully as the big horse continued its steady gait.

"I guess it was kinda dumb of me to ride him," Joey called out.

"I guess," Barry responded. "But you didn't know any better. Mr. Hanson said you did real good. I wish I could have seen it."

Joey chuckled. "Don't ask for a repeat performance. I'm happy to have you teach that critter a thing or two before I hop back on him."

The wrangler looked up in surprise. "You mean you're willing to ride Tar Boy again?"

"Sure," Joey said. "If you'll teach me."

Barry smiled over at the boy straddling the fence. "Good for you, Joey," he called. "You'll make a terrific cowboy, even though you do talk funny."

The New Yorker laughed. "So you don't like my accent? Well, maybe I ride better than I talk, eh, Barry?"

"Yeah," the wrangler chuckled. "Maybe so."

Joey sat silent for a minute, then said, "You know, I was thinkin'. Maybe you could teach me other stuff too, like, how to clean the horses' hooves, and brush them down after a ride, and, I don't know, whatever needs to be done."

Tar Boy slowed to a stop and Barry walked over to the big animal. Every movement the wrangler made was unhurried, carefully planned. He held the coil of rope where Tar Boy could see it as he reached up and adjusted the harness buckle.

"Sounds good to me," Barry said, circling the big animal, the tether held loosely in his hand. "Working

131

around horses is easy once you learn how to think like a horse. If you try to think too much like a human, the animal won't understand what's going on."

The man gently brushed the rope against Tar Boy's sides and legs. He continually ran his hand along the horse's smooth skin, speaking softly to the animal and making quiet clicking noises with his tongue.

"Take Tar Boy here, for instance," he called over to Joey. "I know that he's not used to having people touch him, so I'm showing him it's OK. You took him totally by surprise yesterday. He didn't know what was happening. When you slapped him with the strap, well, that was the last straw.

"You see," wrangler Barry continued, "the more time I spend close to Tar Boy, the more at ease he'll be when I put a saddle on his back.

"All this is necessary before I try climbing on board for a ride. You sort of gave ol' Tar Boy a short course on humans the other day. That didn't work out too good. I'm letting him learn about us slowly, so he'll understand we're not going to hurt him or make him feel uncomfortable."

Joey nodded thoughtfully. "That makes sense. It took me a while before I'd trust Mr. Hanson back in New York. But he didn't let me down. And I really appreciate that."

"Did you have a lot of friends in the city?" Barry asked, running his hand along the horse's neck.

"Nah," Joey responded. "My best friend was my neighbor, Dizzy. She and I sort of watched out for each other. And we had little Samantha, too. When you take care of something, it makes it kinda special, you know?"

The wrangler nodded. "So now you want to take care of horses?"

Joey studied the pasture and the mountains beyond. "I want to be somebody worthwhile, like Mr. Hanson, and Dizzy, and you, too. I want to learn how to do that."

Barry walked over and stood by the fence. "That's a very mature attitude, Joey," he said. "I don't know if I'm the greatest role model in the world, but I do love animals. I'll be happy to teach you what I've learned."

The wrangler paused. "And I think we're going to be good friends." He held up his hand. "Welcome to the wonderful world of horses."

A broad smile creased the city boy's face. He took the outstretched hand in his and gave it a firm shake. "You and me," he said. "We're partners."

"Partners," Barry agreed with a grin.

From the station porch, Grandpa Hanson saw the friendly handshake at the pasture gate. He nodded. It seemed Barry Gordon not only knew horses, he understood people as well.

In the days that followed, the wrangler worked hard, slowly helping Tar Boy regain his shattered confidence in the human race.

The big animal grew to trust the gentle touch of both Barry and the ever-present Joey. Little by little, Tar Boy allowed greater liberties to be taken.

Soon the saddle blanket was introduced, then the big saddle itself. Around and around the horse trotted, wearing the leather apparatus he'd found so distasteful the afternoon he and Joey had made their thrilling dash to the canyon.

The moment finally arrived when Barry felt Tar Boy was ready for a person to be introduced on his back again.

The whole ranch family gathered at the gate, all eyes on the young wrangler and the big black horse.

Slowly, carefully, Barry eased up onto Tar Boy's back. The animal shook its head from side to side and snorted loudly. Barry talked to him constantly, assuring the nervous steed there was nothing to fear.

Suddenly, Tar Boy rose off the ground, his back arched. He ran, leaping and bouncing across the barnyard. Grandpa hollered, "Ride 'im, Barry. Stay with him, son!"

The wrangler held one hand high above his head as the other gripped the saddle tightly. Up and down, back and forth the beautiful animal went.

Barry remained on the rebounding horse's back. No matter how hard Tar Boy tried to dislodge him, he just tightened his hold and stuck to the animal like glue.

Dust stirred up by the pounding hooves swirled around the dancing horse. The crowd watching at the gate was amazed that such a large animal could move so quickly.

Then, just as suddenly as it had begun, the action ceased. Tar Boy stood sweating and snorting out in the barnyard. Joey noticed the fearful look had left the animal's dark eyes. In its place was a firm resolve, a wise acceptance of the man sitting on his back.

Barry bent forward and patted the long, curving neck affectionately. "That's right, Tar Boy," the group at the fence heard the out-of-breath wrangler say, "Everything's OK. We're partners, you and me. We can work together from now on."

Joey recognized the meaning behind his friend's words. People and animals become partners when they start understanding each other.

The young boy glanced over his shoulder at the station, standing tall and proud against the hill. Then he studied the happy faces of his adopted family by the gate.

Realization flooded his mind like the morning sun after a moonless night. That was the powerful potential of Shadow Creek Ranch. Grandpa and Mr. Hanson wanted to help young people begin to understand themselves and others. If they could do that, they'd accomplish something wonderful in the lives of those who came to the little valley nestled in the Montana mountains.

Joey climbed down from the fence and walked over to where Grandpa Hanson and his son stood. "I want to tell you guys something," he said.

The old man smiled. "What is it, Joey?"

"I think I know what you're trying to do here on the ranch," the boy confided. "It's really great. I just want you to know you can count on me to help. I understand street kids. I am one. And I'm beginning to learn stuff about life, and about people, things I never knew before."

Joey paused, then continued. "Mr. H, you didn't give up on me, even when I did stupid things. And Grandpa Hanson, you didn't know me, yet you let me and Sam come here and live on your ranch.

"It's like Dizzy told me a million times. 'Joey,' she said, 'not everyone is bad. There are just bad situations good people don't know how to handle yet.' I think you want to teach people like me how to handle bad situations.

"I never had nobody, other than Dizzy, care for me so much. I feel like I'm the luckiest guy in the world."

Joey's voice trembled as he spoke. "I don't know how to thank you for what you've done."

Grandpa Hanson slipped his arm around the young boy's shoulders. "Joey," he said softly, "you don't know how happy we are to hear you say what you just said. Both my son and I got tired of seeing so much hurt and pain in the world. We wanted to do something about it. Your kind words give us hope that we're on the right track.

"Not only do we want your help, Joey, we need it desperately. You've experienced the streets firsthand. You'll be able to encourage others who'll be coming from that same situation."

The old man paused as if deep in thought. "You know," he said slowly, "all this reminds me of Jesus, God's Son. He came to this ugly world so He'd understand what we're going through, so He'd know how we feel inside. He wanted a face-to-face relationship with people."

Joey nodded. "I don't know much about Jesus, but it sounds like He wanted to be a partner, too."

Grandpa smiled. "Yeah. That's exactly what He wanted to do."

With a thunder of hooves, wrangler Barry rode up to the fence, sitting proudly atop Tar Boy's big back. "I think we finally got through to this old nag," he called, patting the beautiful animal's neck. "He's going to be a fantastic riding horse."

The cowboy looked over at Joey and winked. "Amazing what a little understanding will do."

Joey smiled and waved as the wrangler turned the horse toward the open pasture and raced out across the grassland. The teenager felt a happiness deep inside. Not only had he left the city far behind, he now had a purpose for his young life. He was going to be part of a partnership, an all-out attempt to help kids just like himself.

To the young boy from New York, the ranch represented not only an escape, it was a new opportunity as well. He walked a few paces along the fence and looked out over the green pasture. His thoughts returned once again to the dirty street where he used to live. Oh, if only he could talk to Dizzy. She'd clap her hands together and smile that warm smile he'd seen light up his darkest days.

A tear slid down the young boy's cheek. Turning toward the eastern mountains, he spoke quietly into the wind. "I miss you, Dizzy," he said.

From the gate Mr. Hanson stood watching the teenager. The man nodded slowly to himself, then began walking toward the station. It was time to check in with Martha.

* * * * *

In the weeks that followed, events at Shadow Creek Ranch settled into a comfortable and challenging routine of hard work and exciting exploration.

The children labored at their appointed chores. Grandpa made sure everyone knew what to do. Grandma kept the big family fed; and wrangler Barry visited each Sunday, training Debbie, Wendy, and Joey in the fine art of horse care.

To everyone's surprise, Debbie took to riding as if she'd been born in a saddle. Wendy's pace was a little slower, but steady. Her precious Early was patient and gentle, just like Grandpa knew he'd be.

No one was surprised when Joey announced that Tar Boy would be his official steed. The two energetic animals, one human, one horse, quickly formed a strong bond, despite their rather adventuresome introduction to each other.

Mr. Hanson spent most of his days in his big, upstairs office, fingers tapping steadily on the computer keyboard. His partners in the big city far beyond the distant mountains appreciated the many pages of research their unseen coworker sent through his electronic connection with Martha.

For little Samantha, life in the valley brought unimagined discoveries. Every leaf and bug within reach came under acute scrutiny. She tagged along behind Wendy wherever she went. But, no, she didn't care to ride a horse, thank you very much.

Time slipped by in a blur of activity. The garden and orchard presented eager hands with a rich harvest of vegetables and fruit. Everyone pitched in to help Grandma prepare the bounty for canning or freezing. The food would be welcomed during the cold winter months to come.

As the family worked, days grew shorter and the leaves of the aspen trees guarding the wide yard changed from their summer green to a vibrant yellow. When viewed against the blue sky, the colors seemed almost alive with brilliance.

Other changes were taking place on the ranch, too. The horses seemed to be growing their own fur coats, as nature altered their hair covering from the thin summer fashion to the thick, soft attire of the approaching winter.

Lines of Canada geese could be seen daily, winging their way toward warmer climates to the south. Squirrels and chipmunks went about their work of gathering nuts and seeds with renewed vigor. Even the broad-winged hawks circling high above the pasture seemed to sense that the world would soon change, and food would not be as plentiful as it was now.

One Sunday afternoon, as the autumn sun hung above the mountains, illuminating the valley with clean, clear light, Grandpa called the ranch family together on the station's wide veranda.

"Folks," he began when everyone was settled, "I want to bring you all up to date on our plans for next summer.

"As you know, we've decided to fix up the north wing for this project. During the winter months, we'll all have work to do inside the station. We want to make our ranch home as comfortable as possible for our special guests."

Turning to the children seated by the railing, he added, "Just in case you've been wondering about school, I've got good news for you."

Debbie and Wendy looked surprised. "School?" they chorused. "We haven't been wondering about school."

"I'll bet you haven't," Mr. Hanson laughed.

Grandpa nodded and smiled broadly. "Well, we don't want our ranch workers to be uneducated. So," he glanced around the gathering for emphasis, "Grandma has agreed to act as your teacher. We've ordered home-school supplies from the State of Montana. They have a wonderful program for us to follow."

Joey looked up in wonder. "We're going to go to school here on the ranch?"

Grandpa nodded. "That's right. Your progress will be carefully monitored by teachers in Bozeman. We'll use one corner of the dining room for classes and study."

Grandma spoke up. "I've been looking over your course outlines for this winter. We'll be learning all kinds of neat stuff about science, South America, and what makes airplanes fly. I'm really excited about it. I hope you will be, too."

The three children looked at each other and smiled. "Grandma," Wendy said, "we're going to be the best students you've ever had."

"Yeah," Debbie and Joey joined in. "We'll study hard. We promise."

The old woman nodded. "Good. I don't mind saying I'm a little nervous about taking on this responsibility,

139

but the people in Bozeman have been very encouraging. They said I'll do just fine. I wish I had their confidence."

Grandpa laughed. "You'll do great, Mother," he said. Turning to the children, he added, "and your students will make sure you do, right?"

"Right," they responded.

"Wrangler Barry has agreed to be in charge of the horses next summer," the old man continued. "We're going to fix up a room for him out in the horse barn. I told him he could stay in the station, but he said he wanted to be near the horses. Now that's dedication."

Debbie smiled to herself. She was liking horses more and more.

At the end of the meeting, as everyone was heading out for their evening chores, Mr. Hanson walked up beside Joey.

"Hey, partner," he said quietly, "is something wrong? You've seemed a little sad the last couple days."

The teenager sighed. "I'm sorry, Mr. H," he responded. "It's kinda personal."

"You want to tell me about it?"

The two sat down beside the splashing creek. Joey was silent for a long moment.

"Tuesday is Dizzy's birthday," he said softly, "and I won't be there to celebrate with her. I always get her a present and stuff." The boy looked up into Mr. Hanson's face. "She won't have anyone to be with her. That's why I'm sad."

The man nodded slowly. "I figured it must have had something to do with Mrs. Pierce. Listen, Joey, I'll tell you what. I'm going into town tomorrow on business. Why don't you come along, buy a nice gift with some of your ranch earnings, and we'll mail it to her with an overnight carrier. She'll get it first thing Tuesday morning, just in time for her birthday. How's that sound to you?"

The teenager brightened. "Hey, that's a great idea, Mr. H. Thanks!" Joey jumped to his feet. "It'll make her day, believe me."

Mr. Hanson watched the young man race toward the station. He smiled. "Yeah, Joey," he said to himself. "It will definitely make her day."

Monday morning dawned bright and cold. The lawyer and the city boy ate their breakfast before all the others, then hurried to the minivan. Soon they were pulling onto the highway that led to the broad Gallatin Valley and the town of Bozeman.

The shopping mall was just opening as they arrived. Joey went from store to store until he found the perfect gift. It was a figurine with two beautiful song birds resting on a tree limb.

"Dizzy loves birds," he told the salesclerk as she carefully packaged the purchase for mailing.

Next, Mr. Hanson drove to the farm supply co-op and picked up some horse feed and a list of items for Grandma.

The two ate lunch in a corner restaurant across from the Hotel Baxter. After ordering ice-cream cones, which made them both shiver as they walked toward the minivan, the visitors hurried out of town toward the airport.

"The airport?" Joey asked between licks of vanilla and strawberry. "Why we going out there?"

"To mail your package," the man stated flatly, looking over at his passenger. "Better service to New York."

Joey nodded. "Makes sense."

Inside the little terminal, Mr. Hanson led his

companion to one of the two airline gates and told him to sit over by the big window while he talked to the man behind the desk about the birthday shipment.

The boy sat watching passengers scurry into the waiting area, their eyes eagerly searching for familiar faces. With admiration he studied the smooth-winged airplane parked outside the thick glass. He'd never been so close to one before. Many had flown over his street back in the city; and the teenager had often wondered where they were going and what it would be like to travel in them.

Mr. Hanson stood talking to the airline representative, occasionally turning and waving in Joey's direction.

That Mr. H, the boy thought. *He sure knows how to get a package through. Who else would go straight to the airplane?*

An old woman emerged from the gateway door and stood off to one side as if confused. Joey glanced at her, then back out at the plane.

Slowly his eyes returned to the woman by the gate. His mouth dropped open as his breath caught in his throat. He looked across the waiting area at Mr. Hanson. The man stood watching him, his face broadening into a warm smile.

The young boy rose to his feet and began moving in the direction of the old woman. She searched the faces of those in the room. Then, she saw Joey. Tears filled her eyes as she lifted her hands toward the astonished teenager. Racing across the crowded room, the boy sped into her open arms.

Burying his face in her shoulder, he cried. The old woman stroked his hair gently, speaking words only he could hear.

"Joey," she said softly through her own tears, "your

Dizzy has come home. The Hansons have invited me to live on the ranch with you. Besides . . ." The woman held the young boy's face in her trembling hands. "Tomorrow's my birthday. I couldn't celebrate without you."

Joey wrapped his longtime friend in his arms, unable to voice the joy filling his heart. His every dream had come true.

As the minivan sped south along the highway toward the mountains and the little valley where a creek sang through the meadow and the air was clean and bright, the boy, the man, and the old woman sat in silence, each lost in unspeakable delight.

To the west, heavy clouds were gathering, bringing the promise of cold winds and deep winter snows to the people and places of Montana. But in the heart and mind of Joey Dugan, there glowed a warmth no storm could touch. He knew Shadow Creek Ranch waited just beyond the bend, ready to open its arms wide and at long last, welcome him home.